101
Support Group Activities

For Teenagers Who Bully

A Leader's Manual
for Secondary Educators
and Other Professionals

David J. Mathews,
Psy.D., L.I.C.S.W.

HAZELDEN®

JOHNSON ◯ INSTITUTE

Hazelden
Center City, Minnesota 55012-0176

1-800-328-9000
1-651-213-4590 (Fax)
www.hazelden.org

Library of Congress Cataloging-in-Publication Data

Mathews, David J., 1957–
    101 support group activities for teenagers who bully : a leader's manual for secondary educators and other professionals / Dave Mathews.
        p. cm.
ISBN 1-56838-838-1
    1. School violence—United States—Prevention—Handbooks, manuals, etc. 2. Bullying—United States—Prevention—Handbooks, manuals, etc. 3. Education, Secondary—Activity programs—United States—Handbooks, manuals, etc. I. Title: One hundred one support group activities for teenagers who bully. II. Title: One hundred and one support group activities for teenagers who bully. III. Title.

LB3013.32 .M383 2002
371.7'8—dc21
                                                                              2002019593

06 05 04 03 02   6 5 4 3 2 1

Typesetting by Tursso Companies

Contents

Acknowledgments

This project is the culmination of many years of work and experience in schools and in facilitating groups with students, school staff, and others. Often, school staff feel pressured on a number of different fronts, being required to educate children while attending to the multiple other issues the students present. Many staff members find this stressful. I hope that this book can help ease this pressure, rather than to add to it, and that it will contribute to the view that there is great hope for all children. It is because of what I have learned from these children and staff members that these materials have been developed. I'd like to take this opportunity to highlight all the people who have directly contributed to this book.

Specific people to mention and honor include Yvonne Pearson, who tirelessly and patiently assisted in the crafting of this book. She listened to my ramblings and framed them in a way understandable to others. I credit the publishing staff at Hazelden with continuing to produce materials that focus on the solutions to violence in schools and in our communities. Friends and colleagues provided me with the education, the foundations of understanding, and the support to become knowledgeable about issues regarding bullying. I want to mention in particular Sarah Snapp and Cordelia Anderson.

During the course of writing this book, I experienced the loss of family members and some close friends. I want to acknowledge and, more than that, deeply affirm the work of my parents (Rodger and Dorothy Mathews), who helped me to be in the position I am and to work in this field. In addition, my birth sister, Paula, whom I found through a search nearly twenty years ago, provided a great deal of affirmation while I was in the process of learning.

Finally, the unending support and love I received from my family—my wife, Teri, and my children, Leah, Andrew, and Lukas—was critical. As I wrote this book, I thought about my children's experiences in school. I strategically sought out the principals of their schools to discuss the staff's readiness for addressing bullying behaviors. While my actions were primarily self-serving—to protect my own children—I believe the results will be widespread. It is important that we all take responsibility and make sure that we connect with school staff, informing them of the skills we have and the ways we can contribute to the schools our children attend.

Introduction

Over the past twenty years, I have had the opportunity to work in public and private schools as both a staff member and a consultant. As a consultant, I have been invited to offer assistance in addressing violence or developing violence prevention programs. This has often been a challenging position. Because I was coming into the school asking staff to focus on this task, many people tended to view me as someone who potentially would complicate their jobs. I learned how much time and effort it takes to build trust and promote investment in a violence prevention program. I also came to appreciate not only the commitment it takes from teachers and others to challenge bullying behaviors and help young people make changes, but also the support and acknowledgment the staff need, as well as the teamwork required throughout the system.

Bullying behavior continues to be at the forefront of educators' minds in particular. Creating a safe environment in which young people can learn is a high priority for most school staff. In order for young people to be open to learning, they must be as unencumbered by outside stresses as possible. Young people worry about their safety between classes. They think about going through the hall and adjusting their route based on how it felt when those tough kids called them names last passing period. These concerns distract students and reduce their ability to take in new and interesting information, ultimately affecting their patterns of thinking, their attitudes, and their behaviors. The reality is that, many times, teachers have very similar fears and concerns.

This book is designed for work with a specific population: young people who are identified as using bullying behaviors. This work must be done in multiple environments, and wherever the groups are held, a systemwide approach is critical. The only way to change bullying behavior is to force the entire system within which the behaviors occur to address them. It is my belief that until some significant fundamental changes occur in how schools and school districts conduct business, there will be a continued increase in the violence and deaths within schools.

I have found it both challenging and time consuming to get a systemwide buy-in for these efforts—from administrators, from teachers, from other staff, and from parents. However, the benefits are well worth the time and effort invested. The critical advantages allowed by a systemwide approach include the following:

- Partnerships among all interested and necessary stakeholders promote an essential healthy culture in the system.
- Partnerships by these same people provide mutual support, empathy, perspective, and opportunities for all staff and especially for the facilitator, which enhances the ability to provide young people with what they need.

- Adults throughout the organization demonstrate respectful behavior, which is important, of course, because role-modeling is the most powerful teaching tool there is. The responsibility for addressing concerns lies primarily with the adults in the partnership—staff, teachers, parents, and other community stakeholders.
- The entire organization holds certain behavioral expectations for the young people and communicates these in a consistent form.
- The bystanders—the vast majority of young people who do not use bullying behaviors and are not targets of bullying—are educated on how they reinforce bullying by giving widespread attention to any fights that may erupt.

When you have a systemwide approach, all staff are prepared and educated on addressing concerns, and all of them can make an impact on young people's behavior as well as on improving the entire environment. You can get supplementary information on developing the systemic context for the group this manual is designed to support. For information on getting the buy-in, building trust among staff, helping teachers or other staff to see this program as an asset rather than a burden, and the nuts and bolts of arranging space within schools or other institutions, fitting into institutional time constraints, and so forth, see the program director's manual of the *No-Bullying Program: Preventing Bullying at School,* developed by Beverly B. Title (Hazelden, 2001).

This book has been developed by way of hundreds of hours of practical application in groups with young people of all ages, contact with parents, and consultation with teachers and other school staff. It is meant to be used in tandem with your existing techniques for addressing bullying behaviors, other violence prevention efforts, and education teaching skills. View this book as one major resource in the collection of bullying prevention materials that is growing in your library. Keep in mind that what worked for me in one situation was not as successful with another group. Part of the art of facilitation comes in reading your audience and shaping the material to their needs. It is hoped that this book will contribute to the development of your art as you work with the young people who can benefit from your help by learning to interact with others in satisfying, productive ways.

I want to at least briefly address the terrorist destruction on September 11, 2001, of New York's World Trade Center, which occurred shortly before this book went to press. These events will forever affect all people in the United States, but most of all children. Regardless of what happens subsequently, the personal safety of children has been affected to a degree not previously experienced in the history of the United States. Children have been traumatized. The attack has left an inevitable effect on our children that we cannot ignore, making them feel more vulnerable and anxious. We have already seen, in the United States, an increase in violent incidents aimed at people of Middle Eastern and Indian descent. The attack will also undoubtedly increase bullying behavior and violence in the schools, and we must be aware of the renewed efforts we must make to interrupt this damaging behavior.

WHAT IS BULLYING?

Most of our current understanding of bullying behavior originates in research in Scandinavia. Dr. Daniel Olweus, a professor at the University of Bergen in Norway, pioneered the early research on bullying. In "Bully/Victim Problems among Schoolchildren: Basic Facts and Effects of a School-Based Intervention Program" (D. J. Pepler and K. H. Rubin, eds., *The Development and Treatment of Childhood Aggression*, Hillsdale, N.J.: Lawrence Erlbaum Associates, 1991), Olweus defines bullying as follows:

> A person is being bullied when he or she is being exposed, repeatedly over time, to negative actions on the part of one or more other persons. Negative actions mean *when someone intentionally inflicts or attempts to inflict injury or discomfort upon another person* [italics added]. Negative actions can be carried out by physical contact, by words, or in other ways such as by making faces or dirty gestures or by refusing to comply with another person's wishes.

My definition—the definition that informs the activities in this book—is somewhat broader: *bullying is any word or action that hurts or threatens to hurt another person or oneself.* I use this definition because I believe that bullying behavior is bullying whether it occurs once or repeatedly over time and whether it is intentional or accidental. However, it is only bullying if there is an imbalance of power. Some of the more common bullying behaviors include physical threats, verbal threats, pushing, shoving, put-downs, name-calling, and intimidation. Bullying can also take a sexual form, which includes making rude and sexually explicit comments as a way of threatening and intimidating someone, or using unwanted touch. And finally, bullying can be direct or indirect—that is, exclusion by a group.

Dr. Olweus identified significant areas of concern for young people who use bullying behavior and for those who are bullied. People who use bullying behaviors tend to have internalized, through their observations and experiences, a narrow and rigid way of approaching the world. They have developed a restricted pattern of thinking that leads them to solve problems in only one way. Generally, they have experienced the short-term rewards of immediate power and control. They tend to lack awareness of choices and empathy for other people.

Counter to what is frequently the conventional wisdom, Dr. Olweus noted that self-esteem was not as large a problem for youth identified as bullies as the other factors. In fact, most of them had a pretty good view of themselves. While this initially seems counterintuitive, I have been surprised, over the years, to discover that the behavior of young people I have known who have been identified as bullies was not based primarily on low self-esteem.

Although young people continue to use bullying behavior because they are rewarded by it, the rewards are short lived and the fallout often negative. The good news is that young people are capable of learning this. Bullying does not necessarily indicate a psychological dysfunction or diagnosis. It is a choice to bully or not bully, and knowing this is empowering for young people. This book is based on the assumption that violent behavior can change; there are alternatives that people can use if they desire to practice new ways of thinking.

It is also important to be aware of the effects of bullying behavior on others. Bullying traumatizes its targets. They report feeling terrorized, sad, rageful, frustrated, hopeless, confused, and powerless, among other things. Many of them develop diagnosable behaviors that reflect anxiety. The result can be lowered self-esteem, inability to concentrate, poor school performance, exclusion from groups, self-defeating behaviors and thoughts, and, in some cases, violent retaliation toward the person who bullied them. The effects on a large percentage of young people who tend to be bystanders and witnesses can also be strong. In addition, when the bystanders take no action to address the bullying, they provide a silent message that reinforces the effects on the targets.

CHANGING BULLYING BEHAVIORS

Basic Program Approach

Addressing bullying behavior requires eliminating the short-term rewards of bullying behavior and helping young people to gain awareness of its long-term and negative consequences. It also requires helping young people to understand that they can have both agency in their lives and connection with others. The activities in this program are structured to help young people gain this awareness and understand that they can have some control in their lives without controlling others, to teach them positive ways of getting their needs met and pursuing their goals, and to build relationships and create empathy.

It needs to be clear that not all children who bully are the same. Each child who uses bullying behaviors does so based on a different balance of factors. So be sure to apply the strategies and activities that fit for your particular group of individuals.

Critical Strategies to Approach Work with Youth Who Bully

Several strategies provide the foundation for working with young people who use bullying behaviors. Organizations that embrace these strategies, and groups that are built on them, will be successful in addressing the needs of these young people.

Building Good Relationships

Research clearly shows that young people who have even one significant caring adult in their lives will fare better, develop resiliency more readily, and find more stability in their lives. Young people who lack an attachment are more at risk for engaging in bullying behaviors (Peter C. Scales and Nancy Leffert, *Developmental Assets: A Synthesis of the Scientific Research on Adolescent Development,* Minneapolis, Minn.: Search Institute, 1999). Thus engaging, establishing, and sustaining meaningful connections is critical to working successfully with children who bully. They are generally caught in a cycle of behavior that sabotages relationships. They do not experience enough of the rewards of connection nor the empathy that comes with relationships. Many activities in this book are aimed at or implicitly carry the message of teaching participants how to be in a relationship and how to build a capacity for empathy. The group process should reflect this as well, building relationships between the facilitator and the participants, and among the participants themselves. As a facilitator, you will find that the relationship you have with a group member or with the group as a whole is often at the heart of what can be used later to redirect, influence, or even change undesired behaviors. These relationships ultimately extend into the wider environment, which leads to the various adults in the system having relationships with the young people that are both real and good.

Establishing a Firm, Respectful Structure

Young people who bully generally can be expected to change their hurtful behaviors only when they do not experience the short-term rewards the behaviors bring. This means that they must be held accountable for their hurtful behaviors. It is important to set a structure within the group that is safe for all participants and to make it absolutely clear that bullying behaviors will not be tolerated. In other words, the group members should be provided a safe and dependable boundary. Clear limits help young people not to feel traumatized over and over by having to guess at where the lines are drawn and help them break cycles that sabotage relationships in their day-to-day lives. When limits are violated, the response should be nonpunishing, and it should provide guidance for reconnecting with the system. Again, this kind of structure must be echoed throughout the system so that young people experience firm, fair limits outside the group as well.

Providing Positive Role-modeling

Young people closely observe the behavior of all of the adults around them. This should put us all on notice that we, as adults, are role models to young people regardless of our age, relationship, or position and status in life. Our behavior influences young people whether we like it or not and whether we believe it does or not. Our behavior is watched, scrutinized, analyzed, and, in many cases, synthesized into the lives of young people. Facilitators have the opportunity to teach by example, to demonstrate that respect and regard must be exhibited by adults and authorities throughout the institutional system.

Relying on Teamwork

It is critical that the facilitator, staff, and parents form an alliance that promotes the ideas in which the rights of others, listening well, and caring are valued and valuable. When the adults develop a team approach, the young people benefit from the role-modeling as well as from the direct support. The staff should provide mutual consultation, feedback, and debriefing for each other and the facilitator. They must maintain continued communication, offering each other the backing to address bullying behaviors as they occur in the group or in the organizational setting.

FACILITATING A GROUP

This book is not designed to teach group facilitation skills. Still, before we look at the special considerations around working with bullying issues, it is worthwhile to review some basic principles on facilitating groups.

Assess your strengths, skills, limitations, and challenges in facilitating a group. Some people seem to be natural facilitators whose instincts lead them in the right direction. Others may be more hesitant. Regardless, I have seen many professionals from a variety of fields learn how to become more comfortable in the role of facilitator. Your increasing experience and comfort with this role can counter those difficult times when you feel overwhelmed by the immensity of the task.

Your role is to help group members to participate. The goal is for group members to talk more and facilitators to talk less. Providing questions and probing for more information allows group members to open up and share their own perspectives, contributing to the overall growth of the group and its individuals. When leading activities, avoid a teaching approach as much as possible. Help participants discover the points rather than telling them. Young people's understanding will be deeper when they arrive at their own insights.

Provide firm guidance. Facilitation and guidance are structured processes. Do not be afraid to exert your influence. Your participation and input is necessary to create the structure that encourages safety for all participants.

Take care of yourself. Those facilitators who burn out tend to experience high levels of hopelessness and doubt that participants will experience meaningful change out of the process. When you encounter high numbers of young people who exhibit bullying behavior, you can become jaded or callous. Seek collegial support and supervision to avoid having the exposure to aggressive behavior affect your outlook on life and trust in others. In addition, looking for ways to broaden your role within the institution where you work can go a long way toward supporting a healthy outlook that will positively impact young people.

I want to share with you some principles I try to remember when facilitating a group of young people:

- It is more important to understand than to be understood.
- The group already has the answers, and usually they are better ones than I could ever come up with.
- Providing observations can be a powerful tool.
- Interventions are built on relationships.
- Relationships are the foundation of helping group members to make progress.

SPECIAL CHALLENGES IN FACILITATING GROUPS

Dealing with Resistance

Resistance tends to show up in several ways. Group members may act bored; they may suggest that an activity is for little kids; they may be silent and offer minimal input or appear sullen and moody; they may be disruptive, refuse to follow directions, refuse to participate, or simply walk out. However, difficult and problematic behaviors should not disqualify a participant from the group. After all, consider the purpose of these groups.

Sometimes, if a participant's developmental stage is inappropriate to the group process, it may appear as if the participant is resisting. The facilitator must determine whether the participant's developmental stage is appropriate.

Remember that resistant members do not have a personal vendetta against you. Their mistrust usually arises out of the ways they have felt treated in the past. Demonstrating to the participant that you care about him or her by your own attentive listening and respectful responses is a strong antidote to mistrust. Here are some ways you can help group members who are hesitant for one reason or another to open up and participate in the process:

- Encourage group members to take part in as much as they are comfortable doing.
- Comment on the participation of the motivated members. Use them as examples, but do so in a subtle way so that you do not set up an unhealthy competition between participants.
- Use past success as a way to guide future problematic behavior ("I remember the three activities you all participated in so well two weeks ago; I'm sure you can continue to do so").
- Focus on the positive behaviors of resistant group members when you observe them, and the resistant attitude will usually begin to lessen.
- Suggest that if a member chooses, he or she can sit out of a certain activity. However, he or she needs to know that you will follow the activity with some sharing and will probably ask for observations and thoughts. Often these members decide to participate rather than become the focus later on in the group session.
- Briefly interrupt the activity and review group expectations or rules about group participation.
- Lead a group discussion asking some of the following questions:

  - What might make it difficult for some to participate in this activity?
  - Is this a hard activity? What makes it hard?
  - Does anyone remember what I said the purpose of this activity was?
  - What information have we learned about the people who have shared so far?

- Have personal contact with each participant and find out who he or she is as an individual. You may wish to have at least one individual session with participants who are very difficult to reach and seek from them a commitment to attend for a mutually specified amount of time.
- Remember, as you are setting limits, that whatever line you draw may be difficult to back up.

Dealing with Aggression

Although rarely, it sometimes happens that a participant will try to hurt someone during a group session. If it appears that a group member is attempting to hurt others during an activity, stop the process and check in with the group members. You may wish to ask questions such as the following:

- How do people feel about the safety of the group right now?
- What is contributing to the lack of safe feelings?
- How else does it affect people when this type of thing happens?

Look for ways to have the individual who has hurt or nearly hurt others talk about what he or she is thinking and feeling right now. Ask this person if he or she will commit to making things safe again so the activity can continue. If the person agrees, continue the activity. If the person does not agree, do not simply stop the activity and move on to another one. This sends a message that the person causing problems can control the functioning of the group. Instead, further group processing may be helpful. Discussing how the behaviors affected everyone helps to address the lack of safety. Modeling the problem-solving behavior also can positively affect the overall feeling of safety in the group; participants will know that the facilitator can be counted on to address issues as they arise. You may need to provide consequences for the person in question; he or she may need to experience sanctions for the hurtful behavior. The discussion described above may need to happen as a way for the person to reenter the group process.

Cultural Competence

The whole area of cultural competence, cultural proficiency, and cultural relevance is not to be treated lightly. Cultural competence means that the facilitator, staff, and parents involved in the system understand the traditions of a particular culture, that they can think with the perspective of the members of that culture. It is more than empathy; it is having an emotional connection to the realities that members of another culture live with. This is different than being color-blind. To say that you do not take into account the color of a person's skin demeans a person from another culture. It sends the message that the other person's culture and distinctiveness as an individual is not important, and the majority culture is the better one.

This issue particularly needs to be addressed systemwide. It is important for staff to be truly invested in building their cultural competence and proficiency. It can be damaging to children of color for staff to simply have a onetime focus on this issue. There are many models currently available to assist staff and systems in addressing these concerns. Seek out a way to address these concerns as well as institutional racism.

Be open in acknowledging the cultural differences within the group. When you point out the differences between group members, it allows for open discussion and assists in alleviating the fears that exist in silence. When no one talks about the fact that there are differences, young people of color feel unsure of what is being assumed about them. These young people are most respected through honest recognition of their differences and then respectful exploration of their stories, journeys, and experiences. I can almost guarantee that if young people are not allowed this process of discussion and exploration, the silence around the differences will explode within your group. This type of explosion can be hurtful and damaging to all the group members and to the group process.

Learn about the different cultural experiences and perspectives of various groups. Waiting until a young person of color participates in your group may be too late. Seek out ways to learn about other cultures that make up the population of your school or other institution. This does not only mean learning more about their traditions; it is also imperative that you gain an understanding of the barriers that exist for this group. What social conflicts are raised when identifying a young person from this culture as aggressive or as a bully? What struggles exist for this group related to language, immigration status, different meanings for words, cultural sayings and valued traditions, and process of development? Knowing this information increases your chance to assist a young person. You do not have to be well versed in every aspect of their culture. You must, however, have practical tools and respectful methods for demonstrating your interest, building a relationship with the students, and becoming an effective role model, even though you are from another culture. You may simply ask a young person questions, such as what their journey to the United States was like, what has been the most difficult part of living in the United States, what traditions exist for them, and what language challenges they might have.

Be careful about the cultural and ethnic balance that needs to exist among the group members. Having members of only one ethnic or cultural group can send a message that these young people are viewed as dangerous, difficult to deal with, and at risk for pushing someone around. If you need to start a culturally specific group (which is valid and is often the most effective manner of bringing together a group of students), it is best to have an adult of that ethnic group be the facilitator. This facilitator should also be afforded the opportunity to shape the activities and the program to match the needs of the groups at this school.

Your Attitude toward Young People Who Bully

Remember that these young people are still children, children who have learned some behaviors that they believe they need but that do not define them. Separate the bullying behavior from the young person him- or herself. The behavior does not mean anything about a young person's core as a human being. This separation is essential to his or her success. It is empowering for young people to know that their behavior does not define them and that they can choose to bully or not bully. This separation also helps keep you from becoming jaded and burned out.

Carefully Considered Language

Avoid labeling young people who use bullying behaviors. Even using the label *bullying group* or *bully's group* will have a negative impact. The label can create extremely difficult barriers to getting support, and it can make it difficult for these young people to change. Such labels will alienate parents, since few think of their child as a bully. The labels will also alienate young people and tend to create an "us versus them" attitude. With labels, the youth may be tagged as unable to learn, as lost causes, as losers, and so on.

Helping Members Believe in Their Ability to Change

People will more often do what they should if they believe that they can. Young people need to feel they have the knowledge and ability to do something before they will try to do it. In other words, you can have the best program in the world for teaching young people to be positive and not use bullying behaviors, but if a young person does not believe he or she is capable of using these behaviors, chances are good that he or she won't. Thus it is important to identify and address how capable the group members feel of trying something different in reaction to a problematic situation.

THE NUTS AND BOLTS OF RUNNING A GROUP

There are many practical questions to answer when you set up a support group. Here are some of the things you need to think about when you are setting up your group:

- **Initial assessments.** I do an individual session with each potential group member before the first group session. I focus on five main areas: personal likes, interests, and dislikes; experience with depression and suicide; past violent behaviors and personal experiences of traumatic events involving violence, loss, or life transitions as he or she identifies them; experience with alcohol or other drugs; and connections to family and other significant people. This initial engagement and connection allows the participant to let down guards and provides more information to use later. Conducting as good an assessment as possible allows for quality service within the group process.

- **The size of the group.** The ideal number of group members is six to eight. This allows each participant to use significant time during each session. However, keeping each participant engaged is the responsibility of the facilitator regardless of the number of group members.

- **The "mix" of the group (ethnicity, race, gender, age).** There are pros and cons to having either a heterogeneous or a homogeneous group. With a heterogeneous group, members are exposed to more perspectives and a broader variety of experiences. A facilitator can capitalize on this by asking members their perspectives on a regular basis. The downside is that many times youth from nonmajority cultures feel isolated and tokenized. Too much difference in age can be problematic because of developmental differences. Mixed gender groups can be especially challenging. Choose carefully the mix, knowing the pros and cons of each. Sometimes you are called upon to do whatever it takes. Be sure to seek the teamwork necessary to proceed.

- **The length of the sessions.** Optimally, the sessions will be one to one-and-a-half hours long.

- **The frequency of the sessions.** Weekly sessions are usually adequate. However, it can also be beneficial to meet more frequently in the beginning.

- **The number of sessions.** The optimal number of sessions is probably between twenty-four and thirty-six, although you can offer an adequate program in ten sessions. One good configuration is to meet three times a week for the first three weeks, then twice a week for two weeks, then once a week for seven or more weeks. In this way, you can start with building strong relationships.

- **The meeting place.** The room should be small enough to promote cohesion but large enough to conduct all the activities. It is also important to meet in the same room, which promotes a feeling of safety for participants. You should also be able to hang pictures or other group creations on the walls.

HOW TO USE THIS BOOK

The activities in this manual are based largely on cognitive behaviorism. This approach focuses on cognitive restructuring or, in other words, reorganizing the way we think about things. The basic premise is that actions are the result of decisions, which are based on feelings, which are in turn based on thoughts. We can alter our actions if we can learn to change the thinking that leads to self-defeating behaviors. Thus the activities rely heavily on role-playing, self-talk, and other cognitive restructuring strategies.

This book is meant to allow you a great deal of flexibility. You can use it to design a program that is tailored to your support group. Some activities that are essential, and these are noted in the section "Constructing a Curriculum," starting on page 13. However, there are many other activities that you can select on an optional basis to fit your group's characteristics, time, setting, and tone.

Organization

The book is divided into four phases that reflect the developmental phases of a support group. The phase number is found in a box at the beginning of each activity. The recommended age for each activity is also located here. However, please note that almost all activities are adaptable for ages ten on up.

Phase 1 is the time when group members get to know one another and build trust. It is the time when they will test you to find out if you can be trusted and if the group is a safe place for them, emotionally and physically.

Phase 2 focuses on increasing the participants' self-awareness and establishing and cementing the connections among participants.

Phase 3 represents a stage when the group feels closer and more trusting. There should be considerable group cohesion at this point. During Phase 3, the group members face the more difficult challenge of learning about bullying behavior, taking responsibility for their actions, and learning how to make different choices.

Phase 4 is when group members consolidate what they have learned and prepare to leave the group. It is a time for reflecting on what they have learned, for summarizing and making safety plans, and for consolidating how they will use their newfound behaviors and insights on their own.

Each activity begins with goals and a short description, which allows you to quickly scan the activity. This is followed by a list of the materials you will need for the activity, if any. Although not specifically listed in the materials section, you should always have a chalkboard or newsprint available. Next are detailed directions for the activity. A "Things to Think About" section discusses a variety of issues related to the topic, including feelings or behaviors that the activities may trigger for participants and that you will want to prepare for. There is also space at the bottom of each activity for you to record your observations. This can be helpful to review before you go into the next session or when you use the book for another group.

Many of the activities employ a "Circle of Courage" process, which is explained in Activity 6. The respect and safety this process provides is very useful in engaging the group members. Participants will become increasingly comfortable with this process as they practice using it.

There are also short informational sections in the book on topics relevant to dealing with issues around bullying, such as assertive communication. These are placed by the activities where the topics are first introduced.

Getting the Most Out of the Activities

1. Always begin by explaining the purpose of the activity and describing the process. Let group members ask questions if they appear confused.

2. Some participants may be reluctant to participate in certain activities, especially in the beginning. Let them know that they can always pass the first time around the circle. Give them a second opportunity when you have been around the entire group.

3. Talk about how each activity went. There are process questions for most of the activities in the manual. Processing helps the participants become more conscious of what they experienced and gain a deeper understanding of what they have learned. It helps you assess what the participants have gained from an activity. It also promotes connections within the group and helps members to feel that the group is a cohesive unit. Finally, it allows you to acknowledge that participants followed through on an activity, which leads to a sense of accomplishment.

4. Summarize the main points of the activity at the end of each activity. This will help the participants understand and remember what they have learned.

5. Offer your observations about the process and group members' reactions to them. This provides them with useful information.

6. Do not force discussion into a rigid mold. I have struggled at times with being able to let go of trying to hear the group members parrot my words back the way I want them to. Some activities just need to be done, discussed a little, and returned to at a later date for more focused discussion.

7. Participants may get wild during activities that involve a lot of movement. If this happens, ask the group to observe and be aware of what happens when this occurs. How do they feel when they watch these sorts of behaviors? What thoughts go through their minds? What do they tend to do initially when these types of behaviors occur? What do they tend to do later if these types of behaviors continue? What would help to reestablish a feeling of safety for everyone?

8. There are a number of activities that involve drawing or other artwork. If group members are self-conscious about performing, assure them they do not have to be able to draw realistically. They are not being judged on their drawing ability.

9. There are many activities that involve role-playing or acting. Some young people find doing this in front of a group difficult. One way to help increase their comfort is to identify one or two of the group members who might be willing to go first.

10. Be mindful of pacing. I use what I call the *Sesame Street* and *Mr. Rogers* combination approach. I begin a session with the high-energy *Sesame Street* approach to energize participants. As the group continues, or if individual concerns are raised, I slow the session down to the lower-key *Mr. Rogers* level so feelings and thoughts can be attended to. I may then return to the *Sesame Street* level. You are in charge of pacing and should use it to keep the participants engaged as well as to allow reflection.

11. Fit the activities to the students, not the students to the activities.
12. Fit the activities to your style. However, avoid being rigid with your style. You don't want to fit the young people to the educational system instead of creatively looking for ways to meet and address their needs.
13. You may have to adapt some of the activities so they fit into your institution's guidelines. Administrators or staff may view some activities as risking liability. None of the activities are dangerous. However, some of the discussions could provoke some controversy among staff and parents.

CONSTRUCTING A CURRICULUM

Most of the activities in the manual are optional and can be mixed and matched to fit your particular group. Some activities will work better with your group than others, and you will undoubtedly find some that simply won't work for some group participants. Be mindful of which activities will be most appropriate. This may mean trying new activities for different groups or modifying activities to meet a particular group's needs. It may also mean that you change the curriculum you initially planned as you work with your group's participants. This flexibility will enhance your style and allow you to stay fresh in facilitating the groups.

There are content areas that should be present in every curriculum that you plan. Activities should be drawn from each of these areas.

In Phase 1

- introducing the group members and establishing group rules and norms
- promoting connections among group members
- helping group members feel comfortable participating

In Phase 2

- sorting out priorities
- promoting self-awareness and an ability to recognize and express feelings
- understanding and building relationships
- helping group members be aware of who their role models are and how these role models affect them

In Phase 3

- receiving information on bullying, the escalation cycle, and assertiveness
- taking responsibility for one's own actions
- learning how to make positive choices
- developing empathy
- developing a concept of peace and safety

In Phase 4

- solidifying what has been learned
- saying good-bye

You can draw on these elements largely in the order of the activities, although there are certainly elements from earlier phases that will need to be revisited throughout the program. For instance, you will use activities all the way through that help participants connect with their feelings and with each other.

While there is room for considerable flexibility, the activities do build on each other, and there are some specific activities that are critical to the program and should be used at certain times in the process.

Activities 1, 2, and 3—Introductions, Group Expectations, and Group Goals—introduce the participants to each other and establish the rules. These are designed to be used in the first session.

Activity 6, Circle of Courage, should be used in one of the early sessions since it introduces a critical process that will be used repeatedly in subsequent sessions.

Activity 51, Defining Violence, Abuse, and Bullying, and Activity 52, Recognizing Signals (which teaches the escalation cycle), both provide essential information for participants and should be used before the other relatively challenging activities that are found in Phase 3.

Be sure to include the following activities as well:

- Activity 55, Being Assertive
- Activity 75, Responsible Behavior Plans
- Activity 76, Healthy Choices
- Activity 95, A Safe Place
- Activity 97, Accessing Support
- Activity 100, What I Learned . . .

These activities help participants understand necessary concepts, expose them to new alternatives, let them practice positive options, help them recognize support systems, and allow them to review the group experience.

Most activities are to be used only once during the course of the curriculum, but there are some, such as Activity 5, Feelings Check-in, that lend themselves to frequent repetition. There are also some that you can spread out over several sessions.

You can fill some sessions with many activities and others with only a few. It is always helpful to have at least three other activities ready to use in case one or more are not working or the group moves through the activities more quickly than you expected. At times when you sense the pace is getting slow or the students are bored, feel free to interject an activity that might not necessarily belong in the agenda but would help to reengage group participants. Try to stay flexible if issues that get raised by these activities get in the way of fully completing an activity or accomplishing your agenda. It is good to have a prearranged structure prepared, but also to understand that you may need to be flexible in how the session ends up.

As you are selecting activities, think about balance between serious discussion and fun, between talking and movement. It is important to provide a structure in which participants can have fun. Just sitting and talking about how their behaviors must change will not benefit them or the group process. Remember, if it seems boring, slow, or confusing to you, it probably seems that way to the participants as well. Using several types of activities to get them moving around helps the group process.

A minimum of ten sessions is recommended to make even an initial impact on changing a group of young people's bullying behaviors. The optimal length of a program is twenty-four to thirty-six sessions. Below is an outline of two sample curricula with activity suggestions.

SAMPLE CURRICULUM FOR A TEN-SESSION PROGRAM

Session 1

Phase	
1	Activity 1, Introductions
1	Activity 2, Group Expectations
1	Activity 7, A Truth and a Lie
1	Activity 3, Group Goals
1	Activity 8, The Big Wind Blows

Session 2

Phase	
1	Activity 1, Introductions
1	Review activities 2, Group Expectations, and 3, Group Goals
1	Activity 8, The Big Wind Blows
1	Activity 9, Eye Tag
1	Activity 10, Perspectives
1	Activity 6, Circle of Courage
2	Activity 15, Which Is a Priority?
2	Activity 16, Group Priorities
1	Activity 5, Feelings Check-in

Session 3

Phase	
1	Activity 5, Feelings Check-in
2	Activity 23, House of Cards
2	Activity 28, I Feel Good about Myself Because . . .
2	Activity 32, Masks of Who We Are Outside and Who We Are Inside
2	Activity 40, What the Perfect Family Looks Like

Session 4	Phase	
	1	Activity 5, Feelings Check-in
	1	Activity 13, Group Knots
	2	Activity 43, Guess Who My Role Model Is
	3	Activity 51, Defining Violence, Abuse, and Bullying
	3	Activity 52, Recognizing Signals
Session 5	Phase	
	1	Activity 5, Feelings Check-in
	2	Activity 44, Role Model Collage
	2	Activity 47, Reputations: The Good, the Bad, and the Struggling
	3	Activity 61, What Is Respect Like?
	3	Activity 75, Responsible Behavior Plans
Session 6	Phase	
	1	Activity 5, Feelings Check-in
	2	Activity 41, Important People to Me
	3	Activity 53, Draw the Anger Volcano
	3	Activity 55, Being Assertive
Session 7	Phase	
	1	Activity 5, Feelings Check-in
	3	Activity 64, Communication with Peers
	3	Activity 76, Healthy Choices
	3	Activity 78, Knowing My Power
Session 8	Phase	
	1	Activity 5, Feelings Check-in
	3	Activity 66, Obstacle Course of Assertiveness
	3	Activity 86, Walking Away When You Can
	3	Activity 95, A Safe Place

Session 9	Phase	
	1	Activity 5, Feelings Check-in
	3	Activity 67, No One Understands This Part of Me . . .
	3	Activity 73, I Just Reacted
	4	Activity 97, Accessing Support

Session 10	Phase	
	1	Activity 5, Feelings Check-in
	3	Activity 96, Building a Community of Peace
	4	Activity 100, What I Learned . . .
	4	Activity 101, Go-around Good-byes

SAMPLE CURRICULUM FOR A THIRTY-SESSION PROGRAM

Session 1	Phase	
	1	Activity 1, Introductions
	1	Activity 4, Sharing My Name with Gusto
	1	Activity 2, Group Expectations
	1	Activity 7, A Truth and a Lie
	1	Activity 3, Group Goals
	1	Activity 8, The Big Wind Blows

Session 2	Phase	
	1	Activity 1, Introductions
	1	Activity 5, Feelings Check-in
	1	Activity 4, Sharing My Name with Gusto
	1	Review activities 2, Group Expectations, and 3, Group Goals
	1	Activity 6, Circle of Courage
	1	Activity 8, The Big Wind Blows
	1	Activity 9, Eye Tag

	Phase	
Session 3	Phase	
	1	Activity 5, Feelings Check-in
	1	Activity 11, How Many Things Can You Use a Napkin For?
	1	Activity 12, Continuum of Experiences
	3	Activity 51, Defining Violence, Abuse, and Bullying
	3	Activity 52, Recognizing Signals
Session 4	Phase	
	1	Activity 5, Feelings Check-in
	1	Activity 13, Group Knots
	2	Activity 15, Which Is a Priority?
	2	Activity 16, Group Priorities
	2	Activity 17, Feelings Tag
Session 5	Phase	
	2	Activity 20, Face on a Cup
	2	Activity 27, Anger Collage
	2	Activity 35, Similarities and Things We Share
	3	Activity 75, Responsible Behavior Plans
	2	Activity 17, Feelings Tag
Session 6	Phase	
	2	Activity 20, Face on a Cup
	2	Activity 34, Boys' Rules and Girls' Rules
	2	Activity 18, Feelings Volleyball
	2	Activity 39, Family Sculptures
	3	Activity 55, Being Assertive
Session 7	Phase	
	2	Activity 20, Face on a Cup
	2	Activity 28, I Feel Good about Myself Because . . .
	2	Activity 25, Feelings Stories
	3	Activity 56, One's Up, One's Down
	3	Activity 84, Pushing Hands

Session 8	Phase	
	2	Activity 20, Face on a Cup
	2	Activity 48, Woogie Woogie
	2	Activity 47, Reputations: The Good, the Bad, and the Struggling
	3	Activity 58, Communicate Assertively
Session 9	Phase	
	1	Activity 5, Feelings Check-in
	2	Activity 44, Role Model Collage
	3	Activity 59, When I'm Angry
	3	Activity 60, When Someone Is Angry at Me
Session 10	Phase	
	1	Activity 5, Feelings Check-in
	2	Activity 50, Mobile of Peace
	3	Activity 61, What Is Respect Like?
	3	Activity 62, Telling When Assertiveness Worked
	2	Activity 25, Feelings Stories
Session 11	Phase	
	1	Activity 5, Feelings Check-in
	2	Activity 49, Music Lyrics and What They Say
	3	Activity 57, The Passive Game
	3	Activity 65, Communication with Adults and Authorities
Session 12	Phase	
	1	Activity 5, Feelings Check-in
	1	Activity 8, The Big Wind Blows
	2	Activity 32, Masks of Who We Are Outside and Who We Are Inside
	3	Activity 81, Choosing to Respond or Share a Fact

Session 13	Phase	
	1	Activity 5, Feelings Check-in
	1	Activity 14, Group Geometry
	3	Activity 80, Tough Times
	3	Activity 82, Writing Group Stories
Session 14	Phase	
	1	Activity 5, Feelings Check-in
	2	Activity 19, Secret Feelings
	3	Activity 71, Mind Talk
	2	Activity 45, Interviewing Someone with Peaceful Behavior Experience
Session 15	Phase	
	1	Activity 5, Feelings Check-in
	2	Activity 18, Feelings Volleyball
	3	Activity 72, The Only Person I Can Control Is Myself
Session 16	Phase	
	1	Activity 5, Feelings Check-in
	2	Activity 22, Feelings Charades
	3	Activity 73, I Just Reacted
Session 17	Phase	
	2	Activity 20, Face on a Cup
	2	Activity 24, Feelings Face-off
	3	Activity 76, Healthy Choices
	3	Activity 83, What Would I Tell a Friend in Trouble?
Session 18	Phase	
	2	Activity 20, Face on a Cup
	2	Activity 26, Matching Feelings with Faces
	3	Activity 70, Draw the First Problem Situation You Were In
	3	Activity 81, Choosing to Respond or Share a Fact

Session 19	Phase	
	2	Activity 20, Face on a Cup
	2	Activity 25, Feelings Stories
	3	Activity 78, Knowing My Power
	3	Activity 79, Peaceful Alphabet
Session 20	Phase	
	2	Activity 20, Face on a Cup
	2	Activity 17, Feelings Tag
	3	Activity 77, Choice Web
	2	Activity 46, Reinventing Reputations
	3	Activity 79, Peaceful Alphabet
Session 21	Phase	
	2	Activity 20, Face on a Cup
	3	Activity 54, Confusion and Frustration Can Be My Friends
	3	Activity 68, Role-play Appropriate Communication
	3	Activity 79, Peaceful Alphabet
Session 22	Phase	
	2	Activity 20, Face on a Cup
	2	Activity 29, Decisions, Choices, Who I Am, and Who I Am Not
	2	Activity 30, Collage of My Life
	3	Activity 87, Barriers to Successful Behavior
Session 23	Phase	
	2	Activity 20, Face on a Cup
	2	Activity 31, My Strengths
	3	Activity 69, Being Heard by Others
	3	Activity 81, Choosing to Respond or Share a Fact

Session 29	Phase	
	2	Activity 20, Face on a Cup
	3	Activity 90, Possible Endings to Impossible Situations
	3	Activity 94, Journey of Peace
	3	Activity 95, A Safe Place
	4	Activity 97, Accessing Support
Session 30	Phase	
	1	Activity 5, Feelings Check-in
	3	Activity 94, Journey of Peace
	4	Activity 98, Support Web
	4	Activity 99, Supportive Adults in My Life
	4	Activity 100, What I Learned . . .
	4	Activity 101, Go-around Good-byes

PHASE ONE

101 Support Group Activities

For Teenagers Who Bully

A Leader's Manual
for Secondary Educators
and Other Professionals

1.
Introductions

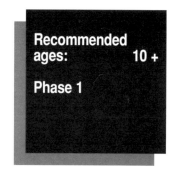

GOALS ▶
- Group members learn other members' names.
- Group members begin to interact with other group members.

DESCRIPTION ▶

Group members introduce themselves and relate various facts about themselves.

MATERIALS NEEDED ▶

None.

DIRECTIONS ▶

Have group members sit in a circle. Explain that it is important for all group members to know each other's name. People are to use first names throughout the time spent together in the group. Ask participants to go around the circle saying their names and one fact about themselves. These facts could include their age, middle name, where they live, or teacher.

When all participants have shared their first names and a fact, ask if any group member can name either all the facts about the other group members or all the first names. You may wish to take the first turn even if you aren't sure you remember all the facts or names. This can be an opportunity to model that adults make mistakes, too. After several group members have tried to recite everyone's name or fact, ask them to say their first names again and name their favorite food. Again, ask for volunteers to repeat the names or favorite foods. You can repeat this process with new categories of facts as many times as you like. Be careful not to do it too many times without changing some specific fact. When this activity is complete, ask each member to say the names of five other people in the group and one fact they know about each of those people.

THINGS TO THINK ABOUT ▶

The first group session and the first few activities can be the most challenging. Whatever you do sets the tone and pace for future sessions. Allow group members chances to pass if they need to at first. However, most students, even the quietest ones, tend to offer something during this exercise. This is particularly true as they feel more a part of the group and hear others contributing things.

MY OBSERVATIONS ▶

_____

_____

2.
Group Expectations

GOALS

- Group members establish mutual working rules for the group.
- Group members glean an understanding of acceptable behavior.
- Group members experience a firm, respectful, and safe structure.

DESCRIPTION

Group members create rules for their behavior toward each other, toward you as the facilitator, and for you as the facilitator.

MATERIALS NEEDED

None.

DIRECTIONS

Explain that it is important for all groups to have a basic understanding of how members would like to be treated in the group. This is done by looking at what we expect from others. Ask group members what you can expect will happen if someone pulls a fire alarm in the school. Look for answers such as the alarm will go off, students and teachers will have to leave the building, the fire department will come to check the building, firefighters will put out the fire. Note that all group members deserve to have expectations regarding how others should treat them.

On a chalkboard or newsprint, draw three columns. At the top of the first column, write "What I expect from other group members." Ask group members to start a list of how they would like the members of this group to treat each other. Look for responses such as these: be respectful, give support, let others talk and say what's on their minds, use people's first names, listen, keep what happens in the group confidential, no put-downs, no name-calling or physical threats, no abuse.

Label the second column "What I expect from [the facilitator's name]." Ask participants to list what is expected of you as a facilitator. Look for responses such as: include everyone, help to make the group safe, help it to be a fun group, start and end on time, don't tell parents and teachers everything that comes up in the group. Note that the facilitator should meet the expectations listed in the first column as well.

Label the third column "What [facilitator's name] expects of me." Look for responses such as these: be on time to the group, allow others to talk, be honest, don't interrupt, be respectful, no abusive language or behavior, no derogatory names or references (and for older students, no using drugs or drinking the day of the group). Also ask group members to use the first names of others or appropriate labels such as *mother, uncle, friend*.

Creating expectations is imperative in this first session. Summarize them into three or four rules. Too many rules encourages "wanna-be" lawyer behaviors and confuses group members. The four essential areas to cover are these:

- Be respectful.
- Use your words to talk it out.
- Work together to solve problems.
- Remember that everyone has the right to feel safe in mind, body, and spirit.

As the facilitator, you get to determine when these rules have been violated. There is no need to discuss violations. The participant is less likely to feel shamed or criticized if you are matter-of-fact when you point out some behavior that is inappropriate.

**MY
OBSERVATIONS** ▶

_____

_____

_____

_____

_____

_____

_____

_____

_____

_____

_____

_____

3.
Group Goals

GOALS ▶	■ Group members develop individual goals. ■ Group members develop areas of focus and purpose for the group.
DESCRIPTION ▶	Group members brainstorm what they want to accomplish during the group sessions.
MATERIALS NEEDED ▶	None.
DIRECTIONS ▶	Ask group members to sit in a circle. Lead a discussion of group goals as follows:

■ Introduce the idea of goals.
■ Ask the group what goals are and why they are useful.
■ Ask the group to choose someone they admire and share what goals they think this person might have.
■ Identify a sport, the purpose behind the sport, and the short-term goals that serve the purpose of the sport. For instance, a baseball team has a vision of winning the World Series. What smaller goals does the team need in order to accomplish its ultimate goal? What smaller goals do the individual members need in order to accomplish the vision? Explain that, like a sports team, this group can establish goals.

Point out that group members may prefer to be someplace else at this time for the next six or seven weeks (whatever the duration of the program might be), but that their presence is for their individual benefit, so it would be good to make the best use of this time. Point out that you can help them do this if you, as a facilitator, have a good understanding of what they would like to accomplish or work toward during the group sessions.

Next, ask participants for their ideas about the purpose of this group. On a chalkboard or newsprint, write goals for reaching this vision. Suggested goals include the following:

- Complete this group.
- Learn how to get mad without hurting myself or someone else.
- Stay out of trouble.
- Avoid the negative consequences that happen after doing something wrong.

When all the goals are listed, ask participants to tell you the similarities among them.

Some students may simply say, "I want to get out of this group." This is an appropriate goal. They can begin to list out loud what steps it would take for this to happen. Participants will probably suggest other goals that you feel are inappropriate. Do not say immediately that the goal is inappropriate. Saying this too quickly can negatively affect the group. Instead, examine what exactly the participant is saying he or she wants from the group by naming that goal. Demonstrate your openness to at least consider whatever they share.

Discussing goals can be somewhat foreign to group members. They may find it a confusing process. The idea of this activity is to expose group members to a goal-setting process.

_____

_____

_____

_____

_____

_____

_____

_____

4.
Sharing My Name with Gusto

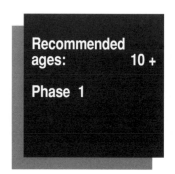

Recommended
ages: 10 +

Phase 1

GOALS ▶
- Group members learn or are reminded of the names of other group members.
- Group members experience increased group cohesion.

DESCRIPTION ▶
Group members share their names along with an action that fits who they are, and the names and actions are repeated by all group members.

MATERIALS NEEDED ▶
None.

DIRECTIONS ▶
Explain to the group that they will take turns saying their first names while doing an action that symbolizes who they are. The group will respond by repeating the name and the action. The group will repeat the response three times. You will cue them each time by pointing to the person. On every turn after the first, the group will go back and review the names and actions of all previous participants in turn before going on to the next participant. Again, you will cue them by pointing, beginning with the person who took the first turn.

Have group members stand in a circle to begin the exercise. Volunteer to go first, demonstrating the instructions by saying your name while doing an action that fits you, then asking the group to repeat it three times. When everyone in the circle has had a turn, you move to the middle of the circle. Point quickly and randomly to participants. Group members should respond by saying each person's name and doing the appropriate action.

THINGS TO THINK ABOUT ▶
Some group members may be hesitant to do an action. You can encourage them by demonstrating an action to go with your own name. Some group members may only shrug their shoulders or nod their heads when saying their names. Even these subtle actions should be used.

As the facilitator, you should encourage members to invent their own unique action; however, if someone is truly stuck, skip over this person and come back to him or her later. When you return to this person, provide some alternative actions to choose from.

Some may try to resist participation in this activity. Your energy and excitement can be a direct influence in full participation.

MY OBSERVATIONS ▶

5.
Feelings Check-in

GOALS	■ Group members recognize a variety of feelings. ■ Group members are able to communicate a variety of feelings they have experienced between sessions.
DESCRIPTION	Group members can begin each session by sharing feelings they experienced during the week.
MATERIALS NEEDED ▶	None.
DIRECTIONS ▶	Have group members sit in a circle at the beginning of the session and share feelings they have had during the week. Begin by stating one feeling you, as the facilitator, had this week and the situation that triggered the feeling. Ask for a volunteer to take the next turn. Continue to ask for volunteers until everyone has had an opportunity to share a feeling. When the turn comes back to you, state how you are feeling right now and what thinking brings you to this feeling. Again, ask for a volunteer to take the next turn, and the next, until everyone has had a second opportunity to share.

The first time you introduce this activity, ask participants to discuss the activity itself when it is completed. Ask questions such as the following:

■ What similarities did you notice among the feelings shared?
■ What similarities did you notice among the thoughts shared?
■ What similarities did you notice among the situations shared?

If you use this activity as a check-in for subsequent sessions, it is not necessary to discuss the activity itself.

THINGS TO THINK ABOUT ▶

Sometimes group members feel hesitant to participate in this activity. Most of them are not used to stating their feelings, much less talking about them at length. It may take some effort on your part to get them to share more information.

Participants may make statements about what they are thinking rather than feeling. When this occurs, gently make an observation similar to the following: "So what you just said was more about what you are thinking when that happened. What feelings were present?" If they cannot identify a feeling, suggest one that you think a person might have in such a situation. You can let a great deal of silence go by, but when you sense that too much time has passed, move the process along.

Remind group members that, at least in the beginning of the group process, no one will be forced to talk. However, you will probably explore further the difficulties in participating with those who stay quiet. You may need to rephrase or reframe what is being shared into a feeling word. You can do this to speed up the sharing process.

MY OBSERVATIONS ▶

_____

_____

_____

_____

_____

_____

_____

_____

_____

_____

_____

6.
Circle of Courage

GOALS

- Group members become familiar with a process that will be used repeatedly in the group.
- Group members feel they are treated fairly in the group.

DESCRIPTION

Group members learn about and practice the process called "Circle of Courage."

MATERIALS NEEDED ▶

A talking piece.

DIRECTIONS ▶

Prior to the start of the session, choose a talking piece that you will pass around during the session. It will indicate who can speak and who will listen. The talking piece can vary from session to session, but it should hold some meaning for you as the circle keeper.

Have group members sit in a circle. Explain to the group that they will be learning a process called "Circle of Courage" and that this process will be used many times during their sessions together. Explain that there are four rules to be used in the process:

- Work at sharing from the heart.
- Work at listening through the heart.
- Work at being spontaneous in your sharing.
- Work at making your contributions brief.

When people sit in a Circle of Courage, they pass a "talking piece." The talking piece is a symbol of the respect that is accorded each person participating in the circle. The person who is speaking holds the piece. All other members are to listen until they have the talking piece. However, explain that, as the facilitator, you will have to provide input to the group process without having the talking piece. Tell the participants that everyone will get an opportunity to share when the Circle of Courage is used. Everyone will also be given the opportunity not to share. The group members who do not wish to share can simply pass the talking piece on to another person.

The talking piece itself will be something you choose, at least initially. Explain what meaning it has for you. A talking piece could be anything from a rock to a stick to a book—any object that is meaningful to you.

Explain that the Circle of Courage is based in Native American traditions. Circles are symbols of some universal concepts and healing processes. The medicine wheel is directly connected with the circle. Have the group practice using the talking piece. The talking piece will be passed around the circle clockwise. Starting with easy responses and progressing to longer ones, ask them to respond to several statements, such as the following:

- Describe a favorite movie.
- Tell what your favorite subject in school is and why.
- Describe a situation when you had a good time with a parent.
- Talk about a time when you made a good decision.
- Share with the group a situation during which you were successful.

Close the process with some ceremonial gesture. This could be simply saying some final words. You as the facilitator might say, "This group will succeed." Or the group could put their hands in the middle of the circle on top of each other, push down, and then raise their hands as they all shout, "Success Together."

THINGS TO THINK ABOUT ▶

This, no doubt, will be a new type of process for group members. Make sure you provide them several examples and allow the group to try out the process several times. Circles sometimes need continued practice by all members.

There are a variety of possibilities for making this process fresh and new for group members. The first few times, follow the procedure of passing the talking piece around the circle clockwise. However, when the group members become more familiar with the process, you can have the person with the talking piece decide whom to pass it on to after he or she is done. Feel free to use your own creativity in coming up with alternative ways to pass the talking piece.

You can also use the talking piece to brainstorm ideas or to collect questions group members might have for others in the group. This helps emphasize that this is *their* group.

MY OBSERVATIONS ▶

_____

_____

_____

_____

_____

_____

7.
A Truth and a Lie

Recommended ages: 10 +

Phase 1

GOALS ▶	■ Group members learn information about each other. ■ Group members participate in the process of sharing about themselves. ■ Group members make personal connections with other group members.
DESCRIPTION ▶	Group members share information about themselves.
MATERIALS NEEDED ▶	None.
DIRECTIONS ▶	Each group member takes a turn stating one fact and one inaccurate "fact" about him- or herself. The other group members then guess which fact is correct. Sometimes it is helpful for the facilitator to list the names and matching truths on a chalkboard or newsprint as they are revealed. This provides group members further opportunity to match names with a fact and improves name recognition of other members. When everyone who chooses to do so has participated, ask participants what similarities exist in the facts that were offered. Help them identify themes in their responses ("Three people shared a fact that was a fun experience," or "Five people talked about a fact that also included a friend or family member"). It is important to acknowledge similarities even when they are only between two or three members. Ask if anyone was surprised by any facts that were shared. Let participants know that focusing on similarities is important. "You are not alone" is a theme that will be brought out in this group many times. It does not mean that they are all the same in every part of their lives or personalities. It does mean that, even with our unique experiences and characteristics, there are ways we all can connect.
THINGS TO THINK ABOUT ▶	Facilitators may be tempted to rush through these early activities to get to the "real" curriculum. Be aware that the early activities are integral to the curriculum because they establish relationships both among group members and between them and you, as facilitator. They also set the tone for subsequent sessions. The group members are constantly observing your actions. They will notice if you are listening carefully and allowing everyone to participate.

Assisting group participants in building their physical, personal, and emotional boundaries is paramount. Many students who use bullying behaviors find it difficult to maintain an internal system of setting boundaries. Here, group members decide for themselves what information they feel safe sharing. In this way, they are setting their own boundaries and asserting their own limits. What they choose to share will signal to you, to a degree, how well they do create their own boundaries. You may find they are sharing stories that might intimidate other participants or offering personal details that make them too vulnerable at this point in the group process. If this is the case, gently break in and remind them that this is a brief exercise, that you want them to simply share a fact. You want to make sure group members do not feel pressured to share information more quickly than they are comfortable doing; trust must be developed on a gradual basis.

Early in the group process, role-model the process of identifying reasons for making decisions. Young people using bullying behaviors often seem to have difficulty breaking down how their thinking leads to their feelings and behavior.

Some participants may use this activity to sensationalize their particular fact or inaccuracy. Avoid allowing this person's agenda to guide the remainder of the activity or the session. Again, gently break in and ask the group member to state a brief fact or inaccuracy. If the member persists, remind him or her of the group's rules and let the member know that you will move on for now, but you'll come back to him or her. You can then ask one of the other members whom you think might be a good role model to take a turn. Provide positive feedback and come back to the other group member one or two people later.

8.
The Big Wind Blows

GOALS
- Group members increase their participation in the group.
- Group members make connections with other members.
- Group members understand some of the similarities they share.

DESCRIPTION

In an adaptation of musical chairs, participants share information about themselves by moving to new chairs when information that describes them is called out by the one group member left standing.

MATERIALS NEEDED ▶

Enough chairs for the facilitator and all group members but one.

DIRECTIONS ▶

This activity is much like musical chairs. All the group members sit in a circle of chairs except for one, who stands in the middle. If possible, you, as the group facilitator, should play the game with the group members. The person in the middle calls out, "The big wind blows for . . ." and then names a characteristic of one or more group participants. The group members who share this characteristic are required to move to a different chair. In the process, the person in the middle sits quickly in one of the vacant chairs. There will be one person left standing. This person repeats the process. If the person in the middle wants everyone to change seats, "hurricane" is shouted.

This process happens as many times as desired by the group facilitator. The facilitator can also direct the types of characteristics being stated. For instance, this activity often starts with obvious characteristics such as shoe color, hair color, or hair length. When in the middle, the facilitator can make this activity more interesting by focusing on concepts and relationships. For instance, it could be stated, "The big wind blows for everyone who was angry this week," or "The big wind blows for everyone who remembers losing something this week," or "The big wind blows for everyone who has a sister." When the game is finished, lead a discussion by asking questions such as the following:

- What similarities did you see in each other?
- What other characteristics would be interesting to ask about?
- What did people notice about how other group members acted before the activity started versus when the activity ended?
- Who seemed to get into the activity most?

The Big Wind Blows tends to build momentum after only two or three rounds. It may begin slowly, but once the participants understand the process, they usually make it fun. This activity builds some playful contact between group members and lets relationships begin that might not otherwise have started. This activity can also produce some excitable behavior. As a facilitator, you always have the option to guide the process to maintain a safe setting.

The movement in this activity is especially useful. It visually emphasizes that group members are not alone because each member who identifies with a characteristic moves. If they happen to be alone in a given characteristic, it is usually interesting rather than embarrassing or shaming. The motion also helps to break down defenses. The physical movement and occasional brushing against each other as participants make their way to their chairs helps to relieve some of the initial tension that exists in the early stages of the group process.

If you, as facilitator, play the game with group members, it tends to be more fun and allows you to provide leadership and role-modeling. The group members take note of the facilitator's actions, and this can be helpful later on in the group process.

There are times when a participant names a characteristic that he or she knows only one group member has. The participant names it and rushes to the other group member's seat when he or she moves. This can turn out to be a playful way of identifying, acknowledging, and accepting differences in others. Should a pattern develop (usually it does not), the facilitator can gently guide a change in the process. You can always create the chance to be in the center by being too slow to get to the last seat. Then, name a characteristic shared by multiple group members. Even as the participants are having fun, they are watching how you respond to situations. As they see you able to guide in a gentle manner, they will build respect for you, the group, and the process.

In those rare instances when a group member calls out an inappropriate or degrading characteristic (e.g., The big wind blows for all fat people), let the person know that this is not appropriate and ask him or her to choose a more positive characteristic. This early in the group process, members learn best through a quick intervention that involves simply addressing the issue and moving past it. This approach sets limits, provides structure, and demonstrates a firm but accepting way to minimize this behavior in future group sessions. As subtle as it appears, the messages you send in this type of intervention are significant.

MY OBSERVATIONS ▶

_____

_____

_____

_____

9.
Eye Tag

Recommended
ages: 10 +

Phase 1

GOALS ▶

- Group members increase their awareness of nonverbal communication.
- Group members increase their trust in the safety of the group process.
- Group members experience increased group cohesion.

DESCRIPTION ▶

In an adaptation of musical chairs, participants exchange chairs when they make eye contact, while the person in the middle races for an empty chair.

MATERIALS NEEDED ▶

Enough chairs for the facilitator and all group members but one.

DIRECTIONS ▶

Group members sit in a circle and maintain silence throughout the activity. One person stands in the middle. When two members of the group sitting in the circle make eye contact, they must exchange seats. While they are in the process of exchanging seats, the person in the middle tries to beat one of them to the temporarily vacant seat. The remaining person goes to the middle to watch for the next two people to make eye contact and exchange seats. This process goes on as long as the facilitator wishes.

Little or no group processing is necessary unless some significant event occurs during the activity. One example would be if someone refuses to participate, or if someone is being too rough. Stopping the activity briefly and asking the group some process questions may be helpful. Only one or two questions are necessary before returning to the activity. You'll want to end this activity while the participants are all having a good time rather than ending it after a negative behavior. This gives group members the chance to change the atmosphere of the group.

THINGS TO THINK ABOUT ▶

Often it takes some time before two participants make eye contact. You may need to be one of the initial people to do so. Once the first exchange has occurred, the process generally gains momentum quickly.

There are usually some participants who avoid any eye contact or movement throughout the process. You can use this information to better understand these group members. Some do not participate because they are feeling peer pressure not to. Some are worried they will not maintain their tough reputation if they participate. However, even those with tough reputations usually make at least a few attempts at playing along. When you are processing the activity with the group, you can raise this issue and observation.

MY OBSERVATIONS ▶

10.
Perspectives

GOALS ▶
- Group members understand that everyone has his or her own perspective.
- Group members gain increased openness to alternative views and opinions.

DESCRIPTION ▶
Group members examine a complex figure in an attempt to identify how many squares it contains.

MATERIALS NEEDED ▶
Copies of the Squares figure (page 43) for each participant.

DIRECTIONS ▶
Explain to the group that we all have our own perspectives on what we experience and what we see. Pass out copies of the Squares figure. Ask them how many squares they see in this figure. Be aware (but do not point out to the participants yet) that the small squares combine into groups to make several larger squares within the figure, which is in itself a large square. After they have all guessed, ask if anyone wants to change his or her opinion. Allow them time to find additional squares. When they seem to be finished, let them know that there are actually thirty squares in this figure. Ask them to tell you which ones they see. Use your finger to trace the squares and help everyone find the squares or groups of squares.*

As part of the follow-up discussion, ask the group if there are sixteen squares in the figure (yes), if there are twenty-one squares in the figure (yes), if there are thirty squares in the figure (yes). All of these answers are true. Explore how they came to see that there were, in fact, thirty squares. Look for responses that support the idea that more squares became evident as people shared their own perspectives. Emphasize that while we all have our own individual perspectives, we can gain from hearing others' views. As a result, we can make better decisions for ourselves.

THINGS TO THINK ABOUT ▶
If there are some students who don't see all thirty squares, do not focus on them. Just mention that it is a matter of perspective. Sometimes group members will get frustrated when other members are unable to see all the squares. Encourage patience. Ask what happens when you see someone having trouble understanding something that you already understand.

MY OBSERVATIONS ▶
_____

*There are sixteen individual squares; there are nine squares formed by combining four individual squares (2 X 2); there are four squares formed by combining nine individual squares (3 X 3); and there is one square formed when all sixteen individual squares are combined (4 X 4).

Squares

11.
How Many Things Can You Use a Napkin For?

GOALS
- Group members increase their ability to see alternatives.
- Group members understand that they can make more creative decisions when they get input from others.

DESCRIPTION
Group members generate as many ideas as possible for how a napkin can be used.

MATERIALS NEEDED
At least three napkins per group member, paper, and pencils.

DIRECTIONS
Pass out a paper napkin and a piece of paper and pencil to each member. Give them three minutes to list as many ways as possible to use the napkin in a neutral or positive manner. They may fold the napkin to help them think of ways. If they have difficulty thinking of more than one or two ways, offer a couple of examples. You might ask if there are ways to use a napkin in the garage or in school besides for cleaning up. Ask each person to share one idea from his or her list without repeating what has already been shared. If they have no new ideas, ask them to pass. Now give them three more minutes to add to their ideas, either ones they heard from other people or new ones that occurred to them as they heard the ones others said. Ask each person how many ideas he or she has at the end of the second three-minute period. Split the group into two separate groups. Have each group compose a list. This list will include the ideas participants had already listed along with any new ideas.

Write on a chalkboard or newsprint all the ideas that the two groups came up with. Ask questions such as the following:

- What were the first two ways you came up with?
- What were the best two?
- How many ways had you come up with when you felt like stopping?
- When did you stop looking for new ways? Why did you stop?
- How did your list increase when you pooled ideas?
- Did some people have a lot more ideas than others?

THINGS TO THINK ABOUT ▶

It may be helpful to use only one napkin as a demonstration model. Then have group members use this same napkin to show how it can be used in other ways. Giving each group member his or her own napkin can waste paper and minimizes the activity.

You can create a story about napkins and in order for the group to survive as a group, members will need to devise a certain number of uses for the napkin.

MY OBSERVATIONS ▶

_____

_____

_____

_____

_____

_____

_____

_____

_____

_____

_____

_____

_____

_____

12.
Continuum of Experiences

GOALS

- Group members realize that each of them has a right to his or her own opinion.
- Group members realize people may see things differently.

DESCRIPTION

Group members move to different areas of the room to visually express their opinions on a list of statements read by the facilitator.

MATERIALS NEEDED

Three signs that read "Totally Agree," "Don't Know, Don't Care, No Opinion, Kinda, Sorta," and "Totally Disagree," and tape.

DIRECTIONS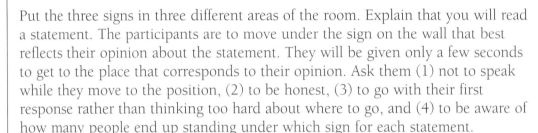

Put the three signs in three different areas of the room. Explain that you will read a statement. The participants are to move under the sign on the wall that best reflects their opinion about the statement. They will be given only a few seconds to get to the place that corresponds to their opinion. Ask them (1) not to speak while they move to the position, (2) to be honest, (3) to go with their first response rather than thinking too hard about where to go, and (4) to be aware of how many people end up standing under which sign for each statement.

Begin with the following list of statements:

- My favorite food in the whole world is pizza.
- My favorite singer in the whole world is _____ (a singer whom the group will recognize).
- I like to rap sometimes.
- I like to come to school for one or more classes.
- My favorite class in school is math.
- I'd rather be hanging out than in school.
- I have at least one other good friend in school whom I feel I can trust and talk to.
- I know at least one adult other than a parent whom I listen to and might even look up to.

Allow your statements to become increasingly situational:

- There have been times in the past week when I got angry at another student.
- There was at least one time this week when I got angry with a teacher or another adult.
- I have strong feelings when someone accuses me of something I didn't do.
- I can remember at least two situations in the past day when I have been frustrated.
- If someone pushes me, I can think of at least one appropriate way to respond.
- I have never seen any violence at school.
- I have seen some violence or have a friend who has seen violence at home.
- There have been times when I have been so angry that I felt out of control.
- There are some other students who bug me so much that I sometimes use violence to get them to stop.
- There are times when it is necessary to use violence in a situation.
- If a boy takes a girl on a date, the boy should pay.
- Men should have the final say in the family.
- Women should only work as secretaries and waitresses.
- When I push someone else around, I feel good at the time.
- When I push someone else around, I feel good later when I think about how I acted.

You may wish to add statements that are specific to the group you are working with. Try to make these statements brief and self-explanatory. Periodically, ask individuals for reasons behind their choices. This is to be done quickly without further processing.

After you have gone through as many statements as you think are helpful, have the group sit in a circle and discuss the activity. Ask questions such as the following:

- Were you ever surprised by how some people answered?
- If so, when?
- What similarities and differences did you notice?
- Were you ever alone in your response during the activity?
- If so, with what statement?
- How did it feel to be by yourself?
- What other issues or concerns might you want to ask about if we had a chance to do this activity again?

End the activity by emphasizing that we all have different opinions. Ask group members what people base their opinions on. Note that for the most part, people's opinions and views are influenced greatly by their experiences and role models.

THINGS TO THINK ABOUT ▶

Be aware that this activity could trigger issues related to peer pressure, other young people's judgments about their opinions, or self-consciousness or shame about an opinion they might hold.

Encourage full participation by group members even though initially they may not take the activity seriously.

MY OBSERVATIONS ▶

_____

_____

_____

_____

_____

_____

_____

_____

_____

_____

_____

_____

_____

_____

_____

_____

_____

_____

_____

13.
Group Knots

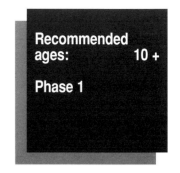

GOALS ▶
- Group members increase interaction.
- Group members feel comfortable participating with each other and in the group process.

DESCRIPTION ▶

Group members create and untangle a human knot.

MATERIALS NEEDED ▶

A clean old sock for each group member.

DIRECTIONS ▶

Have the group stand in a circle. Give each member a sock to hold in one hand. Ask them to offer the other end of the sock to a group member who is not standing next to them. At this point, all group members should be holding one end of a sock in each hand and the group will appear tangled. Tell the group they have five minutes to untangle themselves without letting go of the socks. They are to maintain silence. When they have become a circle again, they should raise their hands in the air. Call time if they have gone beyond five minutes. Lead a discussion, asking questions such as the following:

- What did you notice about this activity?
- Did everyone follow the rules?
- What have you learned about other group members from this activity?
- What was the most difficult part of this activity?
- What was the easiest part of this activity?
- Could you think of any other ways of accomplishing the goal that are easier than what your group did?
- How did the silence rule affect your group's ability to complete the task?
- What was gained by this activity? (Answers might include the following: They can work together even if there are disagreements; there are many ways of communicating; sometimes they need help to solve problems.)

Next, have the group repeat the process, this time being able to speak as much as they wish. Give them another five minutes. Lead another discussion, asking questions such as the following:

- Which method was more difficult?
- What made one way more difficult than the other?
- What is important about communication?
- Who do you know in your life that communicates clearly?
- In what ways does this person communicate?

Many times, group members will have done this activity in another form. Be open to hearing about their other experiences with this activity. Use this discussion as an opportunity to find out what was helpful or confusing before and adjust your approach to the activity and your questions based on the information you glean.

The use of socks or clean rags keeps group members from twisting their arms. They also give group members some distance from each other, which will make the activity safer.

_____

_____

_____

_____

_____

_____

_____

_____

_____

_____

14.
Group Geometry

GOALS ▶	■ Group members experience group cohesion.
	■ Group members learn more about contributing to group problem solving.
DESCRIPTION ▶	The group uses their bodies to make geometrical shapes together within a time limit.
MATERIALS NEEDED ▶	Pictures of each of the following shapes: triangle, square, circle, rectangle, rhombus, cylinder, oval, pyramid, cube, and figure eight.
DIRECTIONS ▶	Post the pictures of geometrical shapes around the room. Group members are to use their bodies to form each of the shapes. The group will form each shape together, and everyone must be included. They cannot talk or make any other sounds while they are forming the shape. When they have completed a shape as a group, they are to raise their hands. They will have three minutes to complete a shape. If they have not been able to form the shape within three minutes, they will move on to the next one.

Once you are sure they understand the directions, have group members stand up. You will call out the name of a shape and give them three minutes to form it. If someone uses words or sounds, remind them of the no-talking and no-sound rules. When they raise their hands after the shape has been made, immediately call out the next shape for the group to create. After they have had a chance to create all of the shapes, have the group members sit in a circle. Ask questions such as the following:

■ What was the most difficult part of this activity?
■ What made the activity easier?
■ What would be different if you could talk?
■ What did you notice about how you developed a way to communicate even though you couldn't use words or sounds?
■ What do you understand about this group after the activity?

THINGS TO THINK ABOUT ▶

Often, it is difficult for the group to stay silent. Some reminders may be necessary. However, if they continue making noises or talking after two reminders, allow yourself to simply observe their process. This information will be helpful observational feedback to the group as you process the activity with them.

Some group members may feel scared or hesitant about physically participating. Let the rest of the group know that it is the entire group's responsibility to take into account these hesitations and find ways to include everyone, but save most of the discussion until after the activity has been completed.

MY OBSERVATIONS ▶

PHASE TWO

101

Support Group Activities

For Teenagers Who Bully

A Leader's Manual
for Secondary Educators
and Other Professionals

15.
Which Is a Priority?

Recommended ages: 10 +

Phase 2 (use in conjunction with Activity 16, Group Priorities)

GOALS

- Group members increase their understanding about setting priorities.
- Group members increase their understanding of how priorities and values are connected to their behavior.

DESCRIPTION

Group members select items germane to their lives from the center of their circle and prioritize them according to the objects' importance in their lives.

MATERIALS NEEDED

For each group member, at least three objects that are germane to the lives of young people, such as a textbook, map, shoe, ball, sheet of paper, calculator, small radio, videocassette, computer mouse, program brochure, comb, bracelet, watch, flower vase.

DIRECTIONS

Have participants sit in a circle around the collection of objects. Explain that, going clockwise around the circle, each person will pick one item. They will go around the circle two more times, then they will have thirty seconds to place the items in order of importance in their lives, with the most important item closest to them on the floor in front of them and the least important item farthest away. This should be done without speaking. When they have completed the task, ask participants to take turns talking about the significance of the items they chose and why they positioned them as they did. Then ask questions such as the following:

- Why did you choose the items that you did?
- Were there similarities in the reasons given for choosing items?
- If so, what were they?
- Why did you position your items as you did?
- Were there similarities in the reasons given for positioning the items?
- If so, what were they?
- If you could have chosen a different item, which one would you have wanted, and where would you have put it?

Emphasize to the participants that everybody has different ideas about what is important to them, and this does not take away from another person's perspective.

THINGS TO THINK ABOUT ▶

This activity may raise issues in addition to setting priorities. Older group members may find the activity threatening. It sometimes touches on core values regarding how members see themselves.

Some group members may be angry that they did not get the item(s) they thought would best fit them. Ask how often they get what they want from others. What happens when they don't get what they want? What do other people in their lives do when they don't get what they want?

MY OBSERVATIONS ▶

_____

_____

_____

_____

_____

_____

_____

_____

_____

_____

_____

_____

_____

_____

_____

16.
Group Priorities

Recommended
ages: 10 +

Phase 2 (use in
conjunction with
Activity 15, Which Is
a Priority?)

GOALS

- Group members increase their understanding of how groups make priorities.
- Group members increase their understanding of peer pressure and its effects.
- Group members experience increased group cohesion.

DESCRIPTION

First pairs, and then the entire group, practice prioritizing items.

MATERIALS NEEDED

See Activity 15, Which Is a Priority?

DIRECTIONS

Do this activity in conjunction with Activity 15. Begin with participants sitting in a circle, each with the objects he or she selected in Activity 15. Break the group into pairs. Have each pair combine their items and prioritize them, again with the most important one closest to them. Allow one minute for participants to discuss their choices and position their items.

Then ask each pair to describe the reasons behind their positioning of the items and the meaning that the items had for the pair. Lead a discussion, asking questions such as these:

- What was the most difficult part of the exercise?
- What was the easiest part of the exercise?
- Did you feel like you had a say in how the items were positioned?
- If so, how did that feel?
- If not, how did that feel?
- Was it a point of conflict between you?

Next, have each pair choose the two most important items in their collections and bring them to the middle of the group. Ask the entire group to prioritize the items that each pair brought to the group. Allow the group ten minutes for this activity.

In the follow-up discussion, help group members explore how this process was different than the exercise they did when they were in pairs. Ask questions such as the following:

- What was easy in this process?
- What was difficult in this process?
- How were decisions made?
- Was everyone satisfied with the result?
- Did everyone feel their opinions about positioning and reasons for prioritizing were heard?
- What might have helped to make this process more efficient?
- What might have made it more effective?

Note that when we make choices with others, we often negotiate and compromise. In other words, we use strategies to get what we want. Sometimes we have to give up something to make progress. Knowing our flexibility level can be helpful in negotiating the best outcome. Discuss this by asking questions such as the following:

- Who do we tend to be less flexible with?
- Our parents?
- Our teachers?
- Our friends?

Explain that having different flexibility levels is a normal and healthy thing.

THINGS TO THINK ABOUT ▶

The intensity of this activity tends to rise as the pairs begin to make their choices. More people seem to engage in the process by the time the group is making decisions. Facilitators often get frustrated with the lack of progress; resist the temptation to take over the process. As the facilitator, act as the observer and group conscience. You may wish to offer observations in the follow-up discussion on how pairs or the group made decisions and whether decisions ever got made.

MY OBSERVATIONS ▶

17.
Feelings Tag

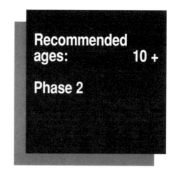

Recommended
ages: 10 +

Phase 2

GOALS	■ Group members increase their awareness of their feelings. ■ Group members increase the number of feelings they are able to identify. ■ Group members increase their understanding of certain feelings.
DESCRIPTION ►	Group members play a form of tag in which the chaser tries to freeze all other group members by touching them while naming a feeling.
MATERIALS NEEDED ►	Copies of the Feelings list (page 61) for each participant.
DIRECTIONS ►	Pass out copies of the Feelings list and review it with group members. Then explain the game of Feelings Tag. One person is the chaser. The goal of the chaser is to freeze everybody in the room. He or she freezes people by tagging them while calling out the name of a feeling. The chaser cannot use the same feeling word more than once. While the chaser is freezing people, anybody who is not yet frozen can unfreeze others by simply touching them while also saying the name of a feeling. When everyone has been frozen, the round is over. Then the last person to be frozen becomes the new chaser.

After doing this activity at least twice, have the group sit in a circle and ask questions such as the following:

■ What feelings used during the game were familiar to you?
■ Were there feeling words used that you haven't heard before or don't know the meaning of?
■ What was the most difficult part of this activity?
■ What made it hard?
■ How did it feel to be the chaser?
■ How did it feel to get frozen?
■ What were you thinking about while you were frozen?

THINGS TO THINK ABOUT ▶

Be clear about structure and limits before group members begin this activity and guide it closely. Act as a referee if a difference arises due to a feeling word that is used. Address the concern quickly and return to the activity.

Clearly define the space that the participants must stay within. Too much space can frustrate the chaser. You may even wish to mark off the area with tape.

When the group members seem to be using the same feeling words, it can be helpful to suggest that the players can use words related to only one feeling, such as anger or sadness or happiness.

Periodically, stop the activity and ask questions of the group that help the members identify more feelings and what they are thinking when they get stuck or need help or just want to quit.

MY OBSERVATIONS ▶

_____

_____

_____

_____

_____

_____

_____

_____

_____

_____

_____

_____

Feelings

(You may wish to have this list posted in the room during all sessions.)

Happy	Pleased	Tired	Full of dread	Dominating	Outraged
Excited	Fortunate	Exhausted	Tormented	Provoked	Fuming
Elated	Blessed	Helpless	Tense	Perturbed	Exploited
Ecstatic	Hopeful	Crushed	Anxious	Aggravated	Spiteful
Terrific	Optimistic	Worthless	Apprehensive	Deceived	Patronized
Jubilant	✳	Disappointed	Threatened	Anguished	Vindictive
Thrilled	Pessimistic	Upset	Uneasy	Harassed	Used
Loved	Cranky	Not good	Defensive	Exasperated	Repulsed
Valued	Bad	enough	Insecure	Irritated	Ridiculed
Appreciated	Sad	Ashamed	Skeptical	Agitated	✳
Enthusiastic	Sorrowful	Disillusioned	Suspicious	Annoyed	Confused
Marvelous	Mournful	Lonely	Shaken	Peeved	Bewildered
Resolved	Unloved	Neglected	Swamped	Controlled	Trapped
Justified	Unwanted	Regretful	Startled	Offended	Immobilized
Gratified	Terrible	Alienated	Guarded	Stifled	Directionless
Encouraged	Demoralized	Isolated	Stunned	Frustrated	Stagnant
Joyful	Condemned	Degraded	Awed	Smothered	Flustered
Cheerful	Pitiful	Abandoned	Reluctant	Disgusted	Baffled
Relieved	Discarded	Sorry	Impatient	Resentful	Constricted
Grateful	Rejected	Lost	Shy	Strangled	Troubled
Proud	Unappreciated	✳	Nervous	Angry	Ambivalent
Respected	Dejected	Fearful	Unsure	Mad	Awkward
Admired	Disgraced	Scared	Timid	Furious	Puzzled
Accepted	Burdened	Alarmed	Concerned	Seething	Disorganized
Alive	Deserted	Panicky	Perplexed	Enraged	Foggy
Amused	Distraught	Terrified	Doubtful	Hostile	Perplexed
Delighted	Miserable	Shocked	✳	Vengeful	Hesitant
Content	Empty	Overwhelmed	Displeased	Incensed	Torn
Tranquil	Humbled	Intimidated	Tolerant	Abused	Misunderstood
Glad	Devastated	Desperate	Dismayed	Hateful	Bothered
Good	Depressed	Frantic	Uptight	Humiliated	Undecided
Satisfied	Hurt	Vulnerable	Cheated	Sabotaged	Uncomfortable
Peaceful	Wounded	Horrified	Coerced	Betrayed	Uncertain
Relaxed	Drained	Petrified	Forced	Repulsed	Surprised
Flattered	Defeated	Appalled	Dominated	Rebellious	Distracted

18.
Feelings Volleyball

GOALS	■ Group members increase the number of feeling words they know. ■ Group members increase their ability to use the language of feelings.
DESCRIPTION	The group plays a game in which it keeps a balloon(s) in the air, stating a feeling when hitting the balloon(s).
MATERIALS NEEDED	Three or four inflated balloons and copies of the Feelings list (page 61) to hang on the wall and to give to each participant.
DIRECTIONS ▶	Ask group members to stand. Make sure they are in an area that is free of obstacles. Then, as facilitator, launch a balloon, simultaneously naming a feeling. Group members cooperate to keep the balloon in the air. A participant must simultaneously state a feeling that has not already been stated in order to hit the balloon. If a group member repeats a feeling or has difficulty assisting the group, the facilitator may touch that person on the shoulder and he or she sits down. This continues until only one person remains.

This game can be made more complex by adding two or three balloons, depending on the ages of the students, or by having group members kneel while they keep the balloon in the air. You may add still another layer of complexity by labeling different parts of the body with different feelings: arm = anger, hand = love, head = fear, and so on. When the facilitator calls out a feeling, participants can use only that part of their bodies to keep the balloon in the air.

It may help motivate participation to have participants compete against themselves. You can time several rounds of the balloon activity and see if they are able to beat their records. After doing this activity several times, have the group sit in a circle and ask questions such as the following:

■ What are the feelings people called out during the game?
■ What feelings were not called out?
■ What feelings do most people know about?
■ Which feelings could use some explanation?

THINGS TO THINK ABOUT ▶

You should monitor this activity closely. It provides group members a good energy outlet. Guide the process and intervene early by addressing even subtle behavioral concerns. Having group members become familiar with more feelings and words to describe these feelings increases the possibility of their use in real situations. Or, if nothing else, this knowledge will help in processing feelings after a problematic situation occurs.

MY OBSERVATIONS ▶

_____

_____

_____

_____

_____

_____

_____

_____

_____

_____

_____

_____

_____

_____

_____

_____

_____

19.
Secret Feelings

GOALS

- Group members increase their feelings vocabulary and comprehension.
- Group members increase their ability to express feelings in a manner that others can understand.

DESCRIPTION

The group plays a game in which participants increase the size of their teams by guessing feelings being acted out by others.

MATERIALS NEEDED

A slip of paper for each group member, each containing the name of a different feeling, and the Feelings list (page 61). The Feelings list can be posted or passed out to all group members.

DIRECTIONS

The participants play a "guessing feelings" game. The object of the game is to form as large a team as possible. People are recruited onto a team if they can successfully guess a feeling that is acted out by a team leader.

First, review the Feelings list, or at least all of the feelings you have written on the slips of paper. Then pass out a slip of paper with a feeling written on it to each group member. Any two people may then attempt to begin a team. One acts out the feeling on his or her paper, and when the other successfully guesses it, they become a team. The acting out must be done without words or other sounds. The "paper-rock-scissors" game* is used to decide who will act and who will guess, with the winner doing the acting. When two people have successfully formed a team, the person who did the acting becomes the team leader. In an effort to recruit a third member, the team leader takes the other team member to approach either a single third person or another team. The team leader and the third person play paper-rock-scissors, and the winner acts out his or her feeling while the other guesses. If another team is approached, the two team leaders play paper-rock-scissors, and the winner acts out his or her feeling while the entire other team guesses. If the single person guesses successfully, he or she simply joins the pair to enlarge the team. If it is another team, the leader of the team joins the team of the actor when the guessing is successful. In the team that lost a member, the next person in line becomes its leader. The approaching, acting, and guessing continues until everyone in the group has been recruited onto the same team.

*Paper-rock-scissors game: Two people each hold one hand formed into a fist in front of them. They raise and lower their fists three times. As they lower their hands the third time, they shape their hands into a rock (hand is a fist), paper (hand is flat), or scissors (the first two fingers are extended while the thumb and the other fingers are curled into the palm). The winner is determined as follows: Paper covers rock, rock breaks scissors, scissors cuts paper.

Then have the group sit in a circle and ask them questions such as the following:

- Which feelings were the most difficult to guess?
- Which feelings were the most difficult to act out?
- What did you notice about how the group guessed the feeling?
- What could make this activity easier the next time?

THINGS TO THINK ABOUT ▶

Encourage the group members to move quickly through this activity. Once they go through the process a few times, they will increase their speed. You may want to tell them that the second or third time they do this activity, you will time them.

This activity helps them become more comfortable with stating new feelings. Having a discussion to define or clarify meanings of some feelings might be helpful.

MY OBSERVATIONS ▶

_____

_____

_____

_____

_____

_____

_____

_____

_____

_____

_____

_____

_____

20.
Face on a Cup

GOALS ▶
- Group members have an opportunity to express feelings in an appropriate manner.
- Group members increase their understanding of a variety of feelings.

DESCRIPTION ▶

Participants draw faces that reflect certain feelings on paper cups.

MATERIALS NEEDED ▶

Four plain white paper cups for each group member, pens, and colored pencils, crayons, or markers.

DIRECTIONS ▶

Ask group members to think of four feelings that they have had in the past two weeks. Have them draw faces on four cups to reflect these feelings. Have them start each face with the eyes, then the mouth, then any other facial feature necessary to demonstrate the feeling. They can color or shade as much as they want. When they are done, ask them to pile the cups on top of each other with their most outside feeling on top, the next feeling under that, the next feeling under that, and finally the deepest feeling they had. Ask each group member to share their cups and the situations behind the feelings. Ask questions such as the following:

- What were some of the similar feelings expressed by group members?
- If you had more cups, are there some feelings you could add?
- How does this process help people share their feelings?

THINGS TO THINK ABOUT ▶

You may wish to use this activity in subsequent sessions, allowing participants to add feeling cups and ultimately to develop a tall collection of feeling cups. Group members appreciate consistency in the activities.

Drawing more feeling cups can also prove helpful in subsequent sessions if participants are reluctant to share feelings.

MY OBSERVATIONS ▶

_____

_____

_____

21.
I've Got a Feeling

GOALS ▶

- Group members can identify multiple feelings.
- Group members increase their ability to identify how others are feeling.
- Group members can ask direct questions to ascertain how others are feeling.

DESCRIPTION ▶

Teams compete to see which team can most often guess the name of a feeling that is written on a slip of paper and drawn by one team member from a container. They guess on the basis of ten yes-or-no questions.

MATERIALS NEEDED ▶

A slip of paper with a different feeling written on it for every group member and a large jar or other container to hold the slips of paper.

DIRECTIONS ▶

Divide the group into two teams. Explain that one person on each team will draw a feeling on a slip of paper from the container. The rest of the team must guess what the feeling is. They may ask ten questions, and the participant who knows the feeling can say only yes or no. They have two minutes to ask the ten questions and guess the answer. If they cannot do so within this time, the other team gains a point. The teams take turns doing this so they can watch each other. Add the points to see which team was able to identify the most feelings. Ask questions such as the following:

- What was the most difficult part of this activity?
- What feelings were harder to guess?
- What made these harder to guess?
- Were there some questions that were more useful than others?
- Which ones?
- What did you learn about how to ask about feelings?

THINGS TO THINK ABOUT ▶

Many participants probably do not have the skills to figure out whether other people's feelings are related to the participant's behavior or not. This activity builds the foundation for participants to learn how to do this so they can stop making assumptions about others.

While there is really no winner or loser in this activity, competing for points helps motivate participation.

MY OBSERVATIONS ▶

22.
Feelings Charades

GOALS	■ Group members increase their awareness of their feelings. ■ Group members increase their understanding of the connection between having and showing feelings.
DESCRIPTION	Participants take turns acting out feeling words while other group members try to guess the feeling.
MATERIALS NEEDED	A jar containing folded pieces of paper with different feelings written on each. A face illustrating the feeling should also be drawn on each piece. There should be at least two pieces of paper for each participant.
DIRECTIONS	Ask for a volunteer to select one piece of paper from the jar. After taking thirty seconds to prepare, the participant pantomimes the feeling. The first group member to accurately guess the feeling word takes the next turn. This process continues until the papers are all gone and everyone has had two chances to perform a charade. If someone who has had two turns gets a third chance, ask the participant to choose someone who has not yet done a charade twice. Lead a discussion using questions such as the following:

■ What was the most difficult part of the activity?
■ Did it get easier or harder as you continued to do it?
■ Were there any feeling words that you had never heard of?
■ Are these feelings bad or good?
■ Have you experienced all of the feelings at one time or another?
■ Is anyone willing to talk about a situation in which you have experienced some of these feelings?
■ Are there some people whom you should never express these feelings to?

Finally, ask participants to go around the circle taking turns naming feelings without repeating a feeling that has already been named by another group member. Continue as long as time permits.

THINGS TO THINK ABOUT ▶

MY OBSERVATIONS ▶

When you are writing out the feeling words for the jar, you may wish to use only feelings that you think will be understood by group members. Tell participants that if they do not know the meaning of a word they have drawn from the jar, you will explain it to them before they act it out.

23.
House of Cards

GOALS ▶

- Group members increase their feelings vocabulary.
- Group members increase their ability to express a range of feelings.

DESCRIPTION ▶

Group members play a game in which they cooperatively build a house of cards. They take turns selecting a card with a feeling written on it, talk about a situation that has or could bring about that feeling, and then add the card to the structure.

MATERIALS NEEDED ▶

Two decks of playing cards with a different feeling written on the face of each card.

DIRECTIONS ▶

Have the group sit in a circle. Place an equal number of cards face down in front of each participant, saving out two cards. Lean the two cards against each other to begin a structure in the middle of the circle. Tell the group that they will take turns adding to the structure to make it as big as they possibly can. The first person selects a card from the grouping in front of him or her, reads aloud the feeling written on the face of the card, and gives an example of a situation in which he or she experienced that feeling or might experience the feeling. If the participant cannot come up with a situation, the other group members are asked to come up with an example. Then the participant places the card on the structure and selects another card. The participant must continue until he or she can share a situation or experience that matches with the feeling on the card.

This continues until all the cards are gone or the house of cards falls. If the house of cards falls, start a new structure.

For groups whose members are eleven or older, it can be fun to also dismantle the structure one card at a time and have them talk about the feeling on the card they have just taken off the structure. If the structure falls while being dismantled, they can rebuild it.

When the activity is complete, have group members discuss their experience. Ask questions such as the following:

- What was fun about this activity?
- What didn't you like about this activity?
- What situations were described that you have also experienced?
- Did you have the same feelings?
- What other feelings might you have had in that situation?
- Were there any feelings that were new to you?
- What were they?

Explain that when people have more ways to describe their feelings, it is easier for them to be assertive and not feel stuck or unable to respond at times that are difficult.

THINGS TO THINK ABOUT ▶

This activity may be good to use after a more active one during a session. It can assist some group members to focus.

Some participants may find it funny or fun to intentionally knock down whatever structure is made. Ask them to be respectful of the group's work in this process. If a group member does knock the structure down, use this opportunity to further emphasize the group rules and expectations discussed in the first group session. You may wish to ask process questions such as the following:

- What does it feel like when something like this happens?
- What goes through your minds?
- How do you keep from doing harm to someone else?
- What do you tell yourself to take care of yourself?

MY OBSERVATIONS ▶

_____

_____

_____

_____

_____

_____

_____

_____

_____

_____

_____

24.
Feelings Face-off

GOALS

- Group members increase their awareness of their feelings.
- Group members increase their understanding of how to express their feelings.

DESCRIPTION

The group divides into pairs and one member tries to guess feelings being facially expressed by the other member of the pair.

MATERIALS NEEDED

Feelings list (page 61).

DIRECTIONS

Review the Feelings list with the group. Then have group members pair up. Ask one person in each pair to pick three feelings to communicate to the other person. The participant must convey each feeling using only facial expressions. He or she may not use any sounds or hand gestures. The other person in the pair has ten seconds to guess as many of the feelings that are being facially expressed as possible. Have them exchange roles when the ten seconds are up and repeat the activity. When both members of the pair have had a chance to act out the feelings, tell them to add up the number of feelings correctly guessed. The top two pairs can then have a feelings face-off by repeating the activity with a different feeling for the rest of the group. At the end of the activity, ask questions such as the following:

- What was the most difficult part of this process?
- What was the easiest part?
- What did you notice about how others conveyed feelings using only their facial expressions?
- How might you express yourself if we did another round of this?
- When is it okay to express your feelings to your peers?
- When is it not okay to express your feelings to your peers?
- Who has influenced you the most about whether you express your feelings or not?
- What are some of the consequences you might receive if you do try to communicate your feelings to your peers (not necessarily peers who are friends)? In other words, what might be the risks?

THINGS TO THINK ABOUT ▶ Some group members may hesitate to engage in the competition suggested in this activity. If so, you may wish to do the activity untimed. The first few attempts at expressing the feelings facially can be difficult. As participants familiarize themselves with ways to demonstrate or express feelings, it gets easier.

MY OBSERVATIONS ▶

_____

_____

_____

_____

_____

_____

_____

_____

_____

_____

_____

_____

_____

_____

_____

25.
Feelings Stories

Recommended
ages: 10 +

Phase 2

GOALS ▶	▪ Group members understand that their feelings are normal for difficult situations. ▪ Group members are able to invent options for expressing feelings.
DESCRIPTION ▶	Group members take turns contributing sentences to develop a story. Each group member must use at least two feeling words in their contribution.
MATERIALS NEEDED ▶	Circle of Courage talking piece.
DIRECTIONS ▶	Using the Circle of Courage process (see page 35), ask each member to talk about a situation in which he or she remembers having a strong feeling. Next, ask participants to go around the circle responding to the following questions. Have them first go all the way around the circle responding to question one. Then repeat the process for questions two and three.

1. If the situation was difficult, how did you get through it?
2. What did you tell yourself?
3. If the situation was positive, how do you remember the situation and the good feelings that came with it?

Explain that the group will now be making up a story together. You will give them a character and the situation that the character is in. The story will be created as you go around the circle with each member contributing at least one sentence. Each participant must include at least two feelings in the contribution. Write on the chalkboard or newsprint all the feelings as they are used in the contributions. Once a feeling has been used it cannot be used in any form in the rest of the story. When the group has completed its story, there should be at least fourteen feeling words on the chalkboard.

Now start another story in the same way you did the first time. This time, the group members must include in their contributions at least two of the feeling words on the chalkboard. As they use the feeling words, circle them. All the feeling words should be circled by the end of the story. When both stories are finished, ask the group if it was easier to make up the story when they were thinking up feelings or when they were using feelings that were already on the board.

Ask them to show you what each of the feelings looks like without making any sounds.

Read each feeling and watch how each person creates an expression of the feeling. Ask questions such as the following:

- Are you unsure of what some of these feelings mean?
- Are you unsure of how to express some of these feelings?
- Can anyone express . . . (the feeling someone says it would be hard to express)?
- Is it more difficult to express certain feelings with some people than with others?
- What makes it more difficult?
- Has anyone ever heard anyone else suggest that you should not express a certain feeling in certain ways?

THINGS TO THINK ABOUT ▶

Group members will probably need encouragement to come up with their story contributions. Some participants may have difficulty following the story line, but this is generally evened out by participants who do follow it. In addition, you can bring the story back into focus if you decide to take a turn.

MY OBSERVATIONS ▶

_____

_____

_____

_____

_____

_____

_____

_____

_____

_____

_____

26.
Matching Feelings with Faces

Recommended
ages: 10 +

Phase 2

GOALS ▶
- Group members increase their feelings vocabulary.
- Group members increase their ability to express feelings.

DESCRIPTION ▶
Participants guess feelings being expressed by facial expression only.

MATERIALS NEEDED ▶
A sheet of paper listing forty different feelings, with enough copies for half the group members.

DIRECTIONS ▶
Have the group divide into pairs and give each pair a list of feelings. One member of each pair will make a face to reflect each feeling on the list. They may not make any sounds. The other person tries to guess the feeling being expressed. They should do as many of these as possible within one minute. Then they switch roles. Have them keep track of how many they guessed within the one-minute time limit. When they have completed the task, ask questions such as the following:

- Were there feelings you had never heard of before?
- What were they?
- Which feelings were the most difficult to express by using only facial expressions?
- Which were the three most difficult?
- Can anyone express these using only facial expressions?
- What else could you do to express these feelings?

THINGS TO THINK ABOUT ▶
This activity should be completed fairly quickly. You may want to repeat the activity several times and have participants change the person they are paired with.

Expressing feelings using only the face can be challenging. Provide ongoing encouragement throughout the process.

MY OBSERVATIONS ▶

27.
Anger Collage

Recommended
ages: 10 +

Phase 2

GOALS ▶	■ Group members better understand what makes up the feeling of anger. ■ Group members identify their triggers for angry feelings.
DESCRIPTION ▶	Group members make collages using pictures that demonstrate anger for them.
MATERIALS NEEDED ▶	An assortment of magazines that can be cut up, paper, scissors, and glue or tape.
DIRECTIONS ▶	Initiate a discussion of the term *anger*. Use probing questions to help group members deepen their understanding of anger. Possible questions include the following:

■ What does anger really look like?
■ Is anger best understood by an action someone takes, or is it just a feeling?
■ What kinds of thoughts are behind anger?
■ How would you describe anger to someone who is blind and has never seen anyone angry before?

Ask group members to look through the magazines and identify pictures that reflect anger. Have them cut out these pictures and make a collage. Encourage them to use only pictures and not words. Allow twenty minutes for this activity. When they have finished, ask each group member to talk about his or her collage of anger. Ask questions such as the following:

■ What were you thinking about as you gathered the right pictures for your collage?
■ Are there some pictures that demonstrate what anger is?
■ Are there some that simply reflect the feeling?
■ What similarities do you notice among these collages?
■ Are there some pictures in others' collages that would fit in your collage?
■ Are there some pictures that you did not include in your collage? Why not?

THINGS TO THINK ABOUT ▶

MY OBSERVATIONS ▶

Participants may have a difficult time identifying all the feelings that go along with anger, but once they begin practicing, this will get easier for them.

_____

_____

_____

_____

_____

_____

_____

_____

_____

_____

_____

_____

_____

_____

_____

_____

_____

_____

_____

_____

28.
I Feel Good about Myself Because . . .

GOALS ▶

- Group members understand how doing enjoyable things can assist in making healthy choices.
- Group members increase their apperception skills regarding problematic situations.

DESCRIPTION ▶

Group members identify activities that make them feel good and some reasons that they feel good about themselves.

MATERIALS NEEDED ▶

Circle of Courage talking piece.

DIRECTIONS ▶

Using the Circle of Courage process (see page 35), ask participants to share good deeds they have done or would like to do for someone else. Then ask them to share the feelings that come with doing these positive actions. List these feelings on the chalkboard or newsprint.

Next, ask participants to name activities they find enjoyable. Have them share the feelings that result from doing these enjoyable activities. List these feelings in another column. Note that they deserve to feel good about doing these activities. Have each group member verbally complete this statement: "I feel good about myself because . . ." Go around the group until everyone has completed the sentence three times. Write down all of the reasons on the chalkboard. Have the group members share what they notice about this list, asking questions such as the following:

- What does it feel like to say these positive things about yourself out loud?
- Is it ever conceited to say these kinds of things? When?
- Are there other positive words or qualities you might use to describe yourself after hearing those that other people used?

THINGS TO THINK ABOUT ▶

It can be helpful to use a form of imagining. Have group members imagine aloud a difficult situation and say aloud the three reasons they identified during the activity for feeling good about themselves. Establishing a verbal link between the difficult situations and their positive characteristics helps participants to internalize the connection.

The main focus of this activity is not to increase the self-esteem of the student who uses bullying behaviors. It seems that their self-esteem is often quite good. However, having them develop positive images and thoughts about their own abilities and worth helps them make healthier choices for themselves.

MY OBSERVATIONS ▶

_____

_____

_____

_____

_____

_____

_____

_____

_____

_____

_____

_____

_____

_____

_____

_____

29.
Decisions, Choices, Who I Am, and Who I Am Not

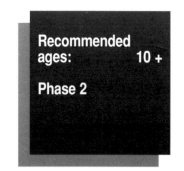

Recommended ages: 10 +

Phase 2

GOALS	■ Group members understand how beliefs about themselves influence their decisions. ■ Group members increase their awareness of how they see themselves.
DESCRIPTION	Participants suggest messages that promote positive self-images.
MATERIALS NEEDED	None.
DIRECTIONS	

Point out to the group that the way people see themselves influences the choices and decisions they make. Give an example of a girl or boy the age of the group members. Tell them this young person was told from a very young age that he (or she) was a problem and was never nice to his parents, to other grown-ups, or to children. He was also given the message growing up that he was so bad no one would ever believe him. Ask group members how these messages given a long time ago might feel to this young person. What might he tell himself when a teacher says he should try to read a book or accomplish another task? How many of these old messages might he retell himself? How might these messages affect what he decides to do?

Then tell the group that the parents got some counseling, and now they give this young person positive messages. Ask the group to suggest positive messages that the parents would be giving now. Then ask group members how these messages might feel. What might the young person tell himself now that he's getting these different messages?

Process this activity by asking questions such as the following:

■ Have any of you heard of a person, perhaps a friend, who got negative messages like these?
■ What sorts of things would you tell yourself if you ever heard these messages?
■ How might you feel?
■ What sort of decision about trying to do something might a person who had been given these negative messages make?
■ How might the negative messages get in the way of trying something new?
■ What could this person say to him- or herself instead to make healthier choices and behave in a more positive way?
■ How would you explain to someone else that how people see themselves affects their behavior?

This activity is not about increasing self-esteem. It is focused on how group members think about themselves based on messages they might have received in their lives.

Sometimes group members have difficulty identifying the feelings they have in response to positive messages. Generally this is due to their lack of experience with genuinely positive messages.

MY OBSERVATIONS ▶

_____

_____

_____

_____

_____

_____

_____

_____

_____

_____

_____

_____

_____

_____

_____

_____

30.
Collage of My Life

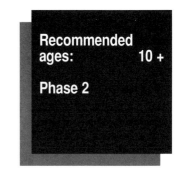

GOALS ▶

- Group members increase their awareness of their individual identities.
- Group members increase their awareness of similarities between people.
- Group members build empathy with others.

DESCRIPTION ▶

Group members make collages that represent their lives and experiences. The collages represent parts of who they are and who they would like to be in the future.

MATERIALS NEEDED ▶

Multicolored construction paper, a wide variety of magazines from which pictures may be cut, glue or tape, and scissors.

DIRECTIONS ▶

Have group members choose a piece of construction paper. Point out that not all of us are the same size or shape, and they may cut their paper to any shape or size they choose. Next, have them look through magazines for pictures that represent five aspects of themselves: (1) their overall personality and outlook on life; (2) two or three significant adults in their lives, such as a parent or teacher; (3) friends and peers; (4) things they do well or feel able to do; (5) a unique aspect of themselves as individuals. Next, ask them to look for three other categories of pictures: (1) some ways they help one or more other people; (2) two or three significant events in their lives; (3) some dreams and future hopes.

Encourage group members to take the time they need to look through the magazines and find the best representations they can of their situations and how they see things. Provide encouragement throughout the time they are searching for pictures and notice as they cut out certain pictures.

When they have selected the pictures, they can arrange them on their custom-shaped paper. Explain that no written words should be used. They may put these pictures on the paper in any order. Point out that collages are meant to demonstrate the overlapping and connected nature of things.

Lead a discussion about this activity while the group members are collecting and arranging their pictures. Ask questions such as the following:

- How did you decide on that particular picture?
- What does it represent to you?
- Is there another aspect that picture represents for you?
- What are the most difficult categories to find pictures for?
- Are there certain words you see being highlighted in the magazines more than others?

When everyone has finished, go around the group and ask them to explain their collages. Empathy is built as each group member identifies with pieces of others' collages. Ask questions such as the following:

- What is the significance of the shape of your paper?
- What is the significance of the color of your paper?
- Can you point to one picture that touches on each of the areas?
- What specific parts stand out in your mind?
- Is there another collage that is very similar to yours?
- What do these collages tell us about people?

When everyone has completed their sharing, place the collages in a connected fashion on a bulletin board or hang them from a hanger in a mobile fashion. This helps to demonstrate that the group is connected. Although there are many differences in many areas, there are still many similarities.

THINGS TO THINK ABOUT ▶

This activity is generally easy for most age groups. The complexity and the amount of information you gain about participants increases with their age and their ability to connect pictures and the areas of their lives. Younger people have more concrete thinking processes and so have difficulty looking into deeper meanings and concepts.

Sometimes young people will fear that their collage will not be good enough. Remind them that their work is not being graded; it is for them.

The magazines they use to collect their images can provide a learning opportunity and lead to a discussion on how marketers market. During their collage assembly, you may help them become more critical of the media by asking group members about who the audience is for certain ads, stories, and pictures.

MY OBSERVATIONS ▶

_____

_____

_____

_____

_____

_____

31.
My Strengths

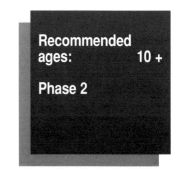

GOALS ▶
- Group members identify their strengths.
- Group members can bring their strengths to mind more quickly and easily.

DESCRIPTION ▶

Group members draw pictures that represent their physical, internal, and external strengths and how they interlock.

MATERIALS NEEDED ▶

Three sheets of drawing paper for each group member, pencils, and crayons, colored pencils, or markers.

DIRECTIONS ▶

Begin by telling group members that there are three kinds of strengths that everybody has: physical, internal, and external. Write the strengths across the top of the chalkboard or newsprint. Ask the participants to brainstorm examples of each and list them as they identify them.

Physical strengths may include playing a sport, playing a musical instrument, singing, or other skills.

Internal strengths may include the ability to take care of oneself emotionally, trusting oneself to make good decisions and healthy choices, and being capable of addressing tough situations and learning from them.

External strengths may include the ability to express oneself in an assertive manner, communication skills, problem-solving skills, the ability to respond to situations rather than react, and the ability to make healthy choices.

Have group members choose a strength from each category and draw each one on a separate piece of paper. Ask group members to show how these three things are linked. The pictures can be as abstract or concrete as they wish. Provide them twenty minutes to draw and ask them to discuss their thinking as they are drawing.

When all the group members have had a chance to complete their pictures, have each one share their strengths and the meaning behind their pictures. Then ask questions such as the following:

- What did you notice about these pictures?
- What were some of the similarities?
- What strengths were predominant?
- In what ways might being aware of your strengths influence how you deal with other people?

**THINGS TO
THINK ABOUT** ▶

**MY
OBSERVATIONS** ▶

You may need to be persistent in helping participants identify their strengths.
This is sometimes difficult when people have not had many positive messages
about themselves.

32.
Masks of Who We Are Outside and Who We Are Inside

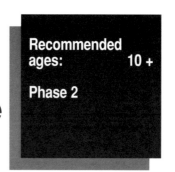

Recommended
ages: 10 +

Phase 2

GOALS
- Group members better understand who they are as individuals.
- Group members better understand how they protect themselves from being overly exposed.

DESCRIPTION
Group members draw faces on each side of a paper plate representing the self they show to the world and the self they keep hidden.

MATERIALS NEEDED
One paper plate for each participant and pencils, crayons, colored pencils, or markers.

DIRECTIONS
Point out to the group that people frequently show one part of themselves to the world and keep some parts of themselves hidden. Ask them to draw their "inside self," the part of themselves that people don't usually see, on a paper plate. Then ask them to draw on the other side of the plate their "outside self," the self they show to the world. Ask them to share as much information as they feel safe sharing. Ask questions such as the following:

- What are the risks if everyone could see the other side of the mask?
- How might this vulnerability affect your relationships with friends? With strangers? With family members?
- How do you think other people use their outside masks to protect themselves?

THINGS TO THINK ABOUT
This activity can produce anxiety. Sharing even limited information that is hidden by the external mask can generate feelings of vulnerability. Continue to assure participants of confidentiality. Also demonstrate sensitivity if participants are reluctant to share what is hidden. Understand that this activity is meant to have limited impact. It provides some support to group members and is best done after the group has some cohesion.

MY OBSERVATIONS

33.
If You Had Three Wishes

GOALS		■ Group members increase their participation. ■ Group members understand other group members better.
DESCRIPTION	▶	Group members identify and prioritize their wishes.
MATERIALS NEEDED	▶	Paper and pencils for each group member.
DIRECTIONS	▶	Ask group members to imagine that they are shipwrecked on a deserted island. They find a mysterious bottle. When they rub it to clean it off and see what the label says, a genie comes out. The genie says they have three wishes. However, there are some things they cannot wish for. They cannot wish for more wishes, for someone to die or be killed, or for someone to fall in love. Go around the circle and ask group members to name their first wish. List these wishes on the chalkboard or newsprint. Go around the circle again and ask group members to name two more wishes and add these to the chalkboard.

Give each group member a piece of paper and ask them to write their wishes on it. Have them number their three wishes in terms of importance. Then ask questions such as the following:

■ Who would you have liked to ask for help in making a decision about the wishes?
■ How would your life be different if these wishes were to be granted?
■ Would there be any negative consequences to having your wishes?
■ Would you share the things you wished for with anyone in particular?

Group members often choose money and specific things. Encourage them to be as creative as possible.

Assist the group members in understanding why they chose the wishes they did and what the consequences might be, especially the negative outcomes.

Allow them to choose wishes again after having heard the contributions of others. The power of this activity can be seen through their process of making decisions individually and then learning from the perspectives of others.

Emphasize that people probably will make better wishes if they hear what others would do with the wishes. Making decisions without the benefit of others' perspectives can be limiting.

MY OBSERVATIONS ▶

_____

_____

_____

_____

_____

_____

_____

_____

_____

_____

_____

_____

_____

34.
Boys' Rules and Girls' Rules

GOALS
- Group members understand how behavior is influenced by role expectations.
- Group members know they do not have to follow traditional roles of men and women.

DESCRIPTION

Group members identify implicit gender rules and discuss their impact and options for change.

MATERIALS NEEDED

None.

DIRECTIONS ▶

Discuss what rules are and what they are for. Explain that not all rules are legal rules. Many rules are developed through tradition, based on how people have believed and behaved in the past. People learn these rules by watching what others do, especially people in their families, and by hearing others' beliefs and expectations. These rules can be hurtful to groups of people and individuals.

Explain that people receive certain messages as they grow up about what it means to be a boy or man and a girl or woman. They are told directly and indirectly that there are certain ways boys and girls should act. Those who choose to act like people of the other gender may be ridiculed. Ask the group members what ways these traditional roles could be hurtful to boys and to girls.

Ask group members what the rules are for being a boy and growing into a man. You may wish to give an example such as having to act really tough. Record participants' responses on the chalkboard or newsprint. Encourage them to share rules they believe are true or ones they have heard are true.

Guide a discussion about these rules, asking questions such as the following:

- How does it feel to look at this list?
- What might a boy do if he heard these messages over and over again in school, at home, or in other places?
- What are the consequences for a boy of breaking these rules?
- Who would give these consequences?

Repeat this process by asking the group to share what rules apply to girls. You may wish to give the example that girls are told to not get angry and to be good by staying quiet. Lead another discussion with questions similar to those above.

Have the group compare the two sets of rules, asking questions such as the following:

- What are the similarities and the differences between the two sets of rules?
- What might happen in the future if boys and girls don't break the rules?
- What might happen if girls and boys do break the rules?
- Who do you think has an easier time, boys or girls?
- If you had a choice, would you rather be a boy or a girl?
- What are the good things boys get that girls don't?
- What are the good things girls get that boys don't?
- What are some positive ways that boys and girls can break some of these rules?
- How might you react differently the next time you see a boy or girl doing something boys or girls are not usually expected to do?

Guide the discussion to help group members understand that these rules are not written down anywhere, and they will not be arrested if they break these rules.

THINGS TO THINK ABOUT ▶

This information lays the groundwork for your ongoing support of group members in trying something new and not following the rules for even one or two decisions in a day. Still, it can be very difficult, especially for boys, when these rules are revealed. Boys tend not to be tuned into these types of influences. They will find it nearly impossible to break these rules.

This activity can also raise issues regarding homosexuality and other related issues. This is an opportunity for you to provide education that allows group members to have a broader and more accepting view of others with different opinions, views, and nonhurtful behaviors.

MY OBSERVATIONS ▶

_____

_____

_____

_____

_____

_____

_____

35.
Similarities and Things We Share

GOALS		■ Group members increase their knowledge about other group members. ■ Group members gain awareness that others have experienced similar situations.
DESCRIPTION		Group members talk about similarities they identify between themselves and other participants.
MATERIALS NEEDED	▶	Circle of Courage talking piece.
DIRECTIONS	▶	Have the group form a Circle of Courage (see page 35) and respond to the following instructions:

■ List two ways at least one person in the group is similar to you.
■ Talk about how it feels to know there is at least one other person in the group who has experienced things similar to what you have experienced.
■ Talk about a time when you have had a friend who understands how you feel because he or she shares similar feelings or perspectives.
■ Talk about a time when you felt alone and isolated even though you were in a crowd.

When everyone has responded, ask questions such as the following about the process:

■ Does it usually feel better to be different and isolated or included and part of a group that shares perspectives or feelings?
■ What similarities seemed to come out most?
■ How do you find out if you share similarities with others in a group?

Summarize your observations of the group's discussion. Ask participants how they feel now that others have heard this information and if anyone is concerned that the information will be used against them.

It can be challenging to get this activity started. It may feel risky to some group members to verbalize similarities they observe among their peers, or they may simply not be used to making such observations. Using the Circle of Courage allows group members a level of safety to share things they might not otherwise share.

**MY
OBSERVATIONS** ▶

_____

_____

_____

_____

_____

_____

_____

_____

_____

_____

_____

_____

_____

_____

_____

_____

_____

36.
Mirroring the Leader

GOALS ▶

- Group members build relationships with other group members.
- Group members gain understanding of how it feels to lead someone else in a positive manner.

DESCRIPTION ▶

Participants practice mirroring each other's actions.

MATERIALS NEEDED ▶

None.

DIRECTIONS ▶

Note for the group that they are going to be pretending they are mirrors. Point out that we can see problems in mirrors such as things in our teeth or pimples that are infected. We can also see good things we do, such as smiling or clowning. Have each group member pair with another group member and decide which of them is going to take the first turn as the leader. Ask the leaders to face you. Have the other half of the pairs position themselves between you and the leader they are paired with, facing their leader. The leaders are to mirror what you do and the followers are to mirror what their leaders do.

Start with simple actions. For instance, raise your right hand above your head slowly. The leaders of the pairs should mirror this and raise their hands. Then lower your hand. Continue to do actions that become increasingly complicated.

After you have done this activity with several actions, have each pair exchange roles. Allow the second person several chances to take the leader role in mirroring your actions. When everyone has had a chance to exchange roles, ask group members to sit in a circle. Ask questions such as the following:

- What was the easiest part of doing this activity?
- What was the most difficult part of doing this activity?
- Was it harder being a follower or a leader?
- What was the most difficult part of being a leader?
- What did it feel like to have someone watch your every move and reflect it back to you?
- What was it like not to do anything that was on your own?
- In what ways do we reflect other people's behavior in school?
- What does being a role model really mean?

Sometimes this activity requires vigorous encouragement for participants to stay with the process. They may be hesitant to follow through because reflecting another person can feel awkward. You can have participants change partners every few actions. This increases the energy. You should also provide participants lots of encouragement even if they are making minimal effort. Start with easier motions or actions, and later in the activity you can have them move more quickly or do two movements at a time. This often brings out laughter. It is sometimes a good practice to point out when they are having fun.

**MY
OBSERVATIONS** ▶

_____

_____

_____

_____

_____

_____

_____

_____

_____

_____

_____

_____

_____

_____

_____

37.
All Tangled Up

GOALS ▶	■ Group members better understand how their decisions affect others. ■ Group members become more connected to each other.
DESCRIPTION ▶	The group members stand in a circle and toss a ball of yarn between them while holding on to the string, creating a web in the circle.
MATERIALS NEEDED ▶	A ball of yarn at least four inches in diameter and a rubber ball or other light ball at least eight inches in diameter.
DIRECTIONS ▶	Have group members stand in a circle. Give the ball of yarn to one group member. Ask him or her to toss the ball to another group member whom he or she feels connected to while holding on to one end of the yarn. He or she should continue to hold the yarn after the second person has caught the ball, keeping the string tight between the two group members. Ask the second person to toss the ball to someone he or she feels connected to while continuing to hold on to the string. Continue to do this until everyone in the group holds the string and a web has been constructed across the circle. You can vary the instruction for selecting the person to throw the ball to. For instance, you may say, "Throw the ball to someone you have been helped by," or "someone who has the same number of siblings as you do," or "someone who has been angry." The person holding the ball of yarn must figure out who matches these statements. The participant may have to ask for information from one or more people in the group in order to figure out whom to toss the ball of yarn to.

Once a web has been created, explain that it is woven from one person to another and all group members have a part of it. Note that this web represents what appears to be a tangled mess. However, it demonstrates how connected and similar all the group members are to each other.

Now ask the group members to count off by twos. Have the "ones" raise the hand that holds the yarn and the "twos" crouch, all of them continuing to hold their parts of the web. Then have everyone stand and be equal again.

Ask the ones to move two steps to their right and the twos to move two steps to their left. Point out the tensions that this change creates. Ask them if they notice what kinds of things happen when people make changes. Guide a discussion about how the group functions when there is tension in some places and not in others, using questions such as the following:

- If some people make changes, does it affect other people? How?
- When someone is angry at someone else in the group, how does this affect the rest of the group?
- If someone does not participate in an activity, how might this affect the group?
- When someone else causes there to be tension, what do you feel?
- What goes through your mind?
- What do you want to do?

Now take a light ball and place it in the middle of the web. Have participants try to move the ball around on the net so everyone has a chance to touch the ball. Let them know they have three minutes to give everybody a chance to touch the ball. Every time they drop the ball from the web they lose ten seconds from the clock.

Lead a discussion about what participants observed, using questions such as the following:

- What made it difficult to move the ball around the group?
- What made it easier to pass the ball?
- What did you learn from this activity about teamwork and understanding how other people do things?

THINGS TO THINK ABOUT ▶

This activity may be too subtle for younger group members. If this is the case, you may wish to ask some of the process questions in a more direct manner.

Remember that participants' experiences with the web bring about insight. You may not see the results of their learning immediately. However, you can continue to recall this activity and its results for them by referring to it as situations arise (for example, when someone refuses to participate in an activity).

If someone refuses to hold the yarn, his or her position can be discussed in the processing time. Ask other group members what it felt like to not have this person in the web, particularly when it came time to pass the ball.

MY OBSERVATIONS ▶

_____

_____

_____

_____

_____

_____

38.
Animal Family Drawing

GOALS

- Group members have a safe way and place to describe their families and some of the problems that may exist.
- Group members increase their understanding of dynamics and relationships within the family.

DESCRIPTION

Group members draw family portraits, using fish to represent the family members.

MATERIALS NEEDED

Circle of Courage talking piece, paper, pencils, and markers, crayons, or colored pencils.

DIRECTIONS

Ask group members to draw their families using fish shapes or types of fish. Explain that this is not a test of their abilities to draw. They can add as much or as little detail as they wish to. When they have completed their drawings, move the group into a Circle of Courage (see page 35) to discuss the pictures. Ask participants to focus their discussion on what the picture depicts. Identify any significant colors, shapes, or surrounding elements of the picture. Have group members describe how they felt while doing this activity.

Next, ask them to show who in this family they are closest to. Ask them to talk about what really connects them to this person. Guide the discussion to assist in revealing some information about how they view their families and their position within the family.

THINGS TO THINK ABOUT

Using animals can be a less threatening way for people to depict their families. Drawing people can be particularly difficult and for some it is important to do it "right." Thus fish are used to represent families. Assure the group members that this is not a drawing contest, nor is anyone being graded for what or how they draw.

You may wish to ask additional questions such as the following:

- How do you see your family in five or ten years?
- Who will be close?
- What types of things might happen to you during that time?
- What other fish or animals might you have used to represent family members?

MY OBSERVATIONS

39.
Family Sculptures

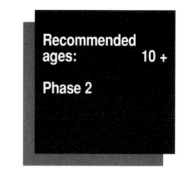

GOALS

- Group members increase their awareness of the differences and similarities among families.
- Group members increase their awareness of how they are impacted by family interactions.

DESCRIPTION

Group members pretend they are sculptors and position participants to represent various relationships within a given family.

MATERIALS NEEDED

Pieces of paper denoting various family configurations: for example, a two-parent family, single-parent family, or foster family, with children of specified ages and genders. There should be as many pieces of paper as there are group members, plus one for the facilitator.

DIRECTIONS

Give each participant a piece of paper with a description of a different family configuration. Keep one family configuration for yourself. Describe for the group the background you have imagined for the family you selected and an experience you have imagined that illustrates how they treat each other. Then ask for volunteers and arrange them in a sculpture that reflects the imagined family's feelings and behavior toward each other. Feelings or behavior may be communicated by proximity, posture, the direction the family members are facing, and so on.

Next ask the participants to take a few minutes to imagine a background for the family configurations they were given and an experience that will show how the family members treat each other. Ask for a volunteer to choose other group members to represent the various family members in his or her configuration. The participant should arrange the family members in front of the group in ways that illustrate how they feel or behave. Allow all group members a turn to do this. Each time a new family sculpture is finished, process the experience using questions such as the following:

- How did you decide to have the people in this family face in the direction you chose?
- Is someone in the family not connected to the others?
- What does this mean?
- Is there anyone missing from this family?
- Who in this family has the most anger?
- Who in this family seems to be needing the most?
- If you could make this family ideal, what would that look like?

When all group members have had an opportunity to create a family sculpture, ask the group what they gained from this activity. Ask them:

- Did you learn anything new?
- Does anyone have a perfect family?
- If there were one way your family could be different, what would you want it to be?

THINGS TO THINK ABOUT

It may be helpful at the beginning of this activity to have some brief discussion of how families communicate with each other nonverbally. Ask them to show you how it might look for a child to feel like the "bad" child when their siblings are given preference, or for a child to feel angry at a parent, or jealous of a sibling, or afraid of a parent.

You may need to guide participants as they build their sculptures. You may wish to ask questions such as the following:

- How does the mom get along with the children?
- How does the dad get along with the children?
- How do mom and dad get along with each other?
- How would it look for the two oldest children to be really angry with the parents?
- How would it look if one of the children felt left out of everything?

This activity may raise intense emotions in the participants that they find difficult to experience and to discuss. Creating fictional families helps them to maintain some emotional distance. Maintain a strong influence in guiding this process so you can help protect the participants from becoming too overwhelmed by their emotions. If you notice some emotional response, explain how this activity can affect others. Let them know that feeling their feelings is okay, and no one will think less of them. Ask the group what they could do to support those who might get emotional.

This can also be a good opportunity to help participants become more aware of their own feelings about their families. However, you should encourage participants to make connections between the feelings in the fictional families and the feelings in their own families only if the level of trust in the group can support the intimacy of revealing difficult feelings and if you feel that you can give participants appropriate support and help them maintain appropriate boundaries. Be prepared to refer group members to other counseling resources if they seem overwhelmed by this activity.

MY OBSERVATIONS

40.
What the Perfect Family Looks Like

GOAL ▶ Group members identify characteristics of a family that are healthy and realistic.

DESCRIPTION ▶ Group members write an ad for a perfect family, identify what expectations are realistic, and discuss ways to achieve desirable characteristics.

MATERIALS NEEDED ▶ None.

DIRECTIONS ▶ Tell participants that they are going to write an ad seeking the perfect family. They have unlimited space and money to pay for the ad. Ask them what qualities and characteristics the perfect family would have. At the top of a chalkboard or newsprint, write: "The perfect family . . ." Underneath this heading, write all of their ideas. Their suggestions may include characteristics such as these:

- has only one child
- is rich
- lives in a house
- lives in a suburban neighborhood
- has no problems
- has perfect children
- has only two children
- has grandparents
- has parents who really show that they love the children

When they have filled the entire board with suggestions, ask which of these characteristics are truly reasonable for any family. Ask the group to identify all the ideas that appear to be absolutes. They probably include the words *always, never, perfect.* Start erasing the ones that clearly cannot be reasonably attained.

When you have eliminated characteristics that are not attainable, have participants identify as a group the five suggestions that they feel are the most important to the health of a family. Ask questions such as the following:

- How do these five characteristics differ from the others?
- Why do some of the characteristics make the priority list and others do not?

Ask participants what a family can do to have healthy characteristics. Begin a list of actions that a family can take in order to work toward them.

Finally, begin a discussion of how their family situations compare to the characteristics of a "perfect" family versus a reasonably healthy functioning family.

Assuming the group has generated a long list of desirable characteristics, it will probably be relieving for participants to know that it is nearly impossible for any family to have all of these.

**MY
OBSERVATIONS** ▶

_____

_____

_____

_____

_____

_____

_____

_____

_____

_____

_____

_____

_____

_____

41.
Important People to Me

Recommended
ages: 10 +

Phase 2

GOALS	■ Group members identify at least one caring adult in their lives. ■ Group members identify one value or piece of information that this important person communicates to them.
DESCRIPTION	Group participants share with each other about people who are important to them and what positive messages these people communicate to them.
MATERIALS NEEDED ▶	Circle of Courage talking piece.
DIRECTIONS ▶	Describe the primary elements of communication: sender, message, and receiver. Explain that this activity will focus on the senders in the group members' lives.

Ask group members to sit in a Circle of Courage (see page 35) and tell one short story about an adult who has been important in their lives. Allow each participant a turn. Next, ask group members to list three direct or indirect positive messages this person gives them. Explain that a direct message is what someone tells them in words and that indirect messages are what someone tells them by their actions or behavior. Some specifics you might listen for include the following: "The adult likes doing things with me"; "The adult spends time with me"; "We can talk about stuff"; "We do interesting (fun, valuable, important) activities together"; "The adult says he or she likes how I . . ."

Write down each of the participant's positive messages on a chalkboard or newsprint. When each person has shared, lead a discussion using questions such as the following:

■ What sorts of feelings do these messages bring up?
■ To what extent do these people provide you with guidance?
■ Do you ever use this person to help you make a good decision?
■ Is this person the best person for every situation in your life?
■ Isn't it interesting how several of you told stories about a parent and some special event or time you spent with this person (or substitute observation appropriate to your particular group). What does this theme say to us?

When group members begin to share the messages, simply record them on the board. Wait until the processing time to comment or ask further questions.

There is often a common thread among the stories and among the roles of the important people identified. This can be highlighted in the processing time. Pointing out these commonalties brings cohesion to the group.

The information that emerges during this activity about themes that concern the group or feelings they experience will be important as you address their bullying behaviors. Having them stay in cognitive contact with the positive and nurturing messages of people who are important to them will provide tools for using more appropriate behaviors in other interactions. This activity is not necessarily directed at issues of self-esteem (although it may have a positive effect on self-esteem). The key issue here is to keep participants cognitively engaged in activities that can result in positive behaviors. If they begin to believe they can use this process, they are more likely to do so.

MY OBSERVATIONS ▶

_____

_____

_____

_____

_____

_____

_____

_____

_____

_____

_____

42.
Collage of Characteristics I Aspire To

GOALS ▶
- Group members identify positive characteristics they wish to strive for.
- Group members understand how others influence their choices and behaviors.

DESCRIPTION ▶
Participants make collages that represent positive characteristics, behaviors, and values, and other group members try to guess what each person's completed collage represents for him or her.

MATERIALS NEEDED ▶
Multicolored construction paper, a wide variety of magazines from which pictures may be cut, glue or tape, and scissors.

DIRECTIONS ▶
Ask group members to think about people they look up to, such as parents, teachers, heroes in sports or the media, or other adults. Have the students identify qualities about these people that they would like to possess themselves. Many times, group members have no experience of the adults in their lives making healthy choices. They may have lived chaotic, stressful lives, and this influences how they view themselves and their world. If participants are not able to come up with examples of positive qualities based on people they know, have them look at some negative ways they have been treated and find the positive opposite. For instance, some students may decide that they will not spank their children. The positive opposite could be that they will respect their children. Write the positive qualities participants identify on the chalkboard or newsprint. Alternatively, you may wish to ask a volunteer to write the qualities on the chalkboard as you facilitate a brainstorming process.

Next, ask group members to cut out pictures and words that represent these characteristics from a collection of magazines. They may use the list on the board to guide them as they clip pictures and words. Have them use the pictures and words to make collages. When they have completed their collages, go around the circle and ask group members to guess the three main qualities each person was trying to reflect. Then ask each person to share the meaning behind his or her collage and the people the collage was based on. Lead a discussion about the possibility of living out these qualities and behaviors using questions such as the following:

- Is it doable to behave in these ways?
- What prevents you from attaining these qualities?
- What might you be doing in ten to fifteen years?
- Do you think you will be showing any of these characteristics at that time?

Group members may need to discuss how a person's behavior reflects his or her values. You may wish to offer the following type of example. John's parents really believed that school was an important experience for their children. Before moving to a new area, they looked at the types of schools and what they offered. The values of the parents guided their decision about where to move.

You may wish to note that none of these people is perfect. Most adults possess considerable shares of both positive and negative characteristics.

Resist the urge to organize group members' collages. Let them do as much of their own organization as possible. If they make placements that make sense to them, it fosters their independence and creativity, and it gives you, as facilitator, more accurate information about how each young person views the world.

_____

_____

_____

_____

_____

_____

_____

_____

_____

_____

_____

_____

_____

_____

43.
Guess Who My Role Model Is

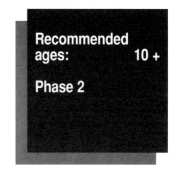

Recommended ages: 10 +

Phase 2

GOALS ▶	<ul><li>Group members increase their understanding of people who influence their behaviors.</li><li>Group members identify characteristics of people they look up to.</li><li>Group members expand their idea of who a role model can be.</li></ul>
DESCRIPTION ▶	Group members play a matching game in which they identify role models and then guess which role model is described by a given list of characteristics or behaviors.
MATERIALS NEEDED ▶	Three 8 1/2-by-11-inch pieces of paper for each participant, three small pieces of paper for each participant, pens or pencils, a container to hold the slips of paper (hat, jar, bowl), old magazines that can be cut up, scissors, glue or tape, and a large piece of tagboard.
DIRECTIONS ▶	Give each participant three pieces of 8 1/2-by-11 paper. Ask them to write the name of a different person (fictional or real) whom they admire on each piece of paper. Have them call out the names they wrote down. Write them on the chalkboard or newsprint.

Then have the participants list under each name on their own papers the characteristics and behaviors that they think are typical of that person. When they have finished this task, ask them to circle on each of the three lists the three characteristics or behaviors that they like the most.

Next give each participant three small pieces of paper. Ask them to transfer the three characteristics or behaviors they circled from each of their lists to the three small pieces of paper. Collect the short lists from the participants and put them in a jar.

Send the jar around to each participant. The first person draws a piece of paper from the jar and reads the three characteristics or behaviors aloud. The group has thirty seconds to match the list to the correct name on the board. Continue going around the group until all of the slips of paper have been drawn. When the game is complete, ask group members questions such as the following:

- Who were the people with positive characteristics picked by group members?
- What similarities were there among these characteristics?
- Are there other similarities among the role models that were picked?
- Was it easy or hard to identify the people by their traits?
- Was it easy or hard to identify who chose this person?
- What helped you figure out who chose this person?
- What did you observe about your choice of role models compared to the choices other people made?

Put each slip of paper on a large piece of tagboard. Then ask the group members to cut out pictures in the magazines that demonstrate or reflect these qualities. Make a collage with these slips of paper and the pictures. This becomes the group collage of role-model qualities and characteristics.

Provide your observations regarding the process and the information that was shared in this activity. Describe a role model you had when you were young. Discuss the role model's characteristics, pointing out which ones were positive and which ones you could realistically hope to attain. Note if there were characteristics that were not possible for you to attain (for example, X-ray vision).

Participants may list superheroes with qualities they cannot possibly emulate. This is exactly the information that you want to gather. It can help group members gain insight and develop useful goals if they can see concretely the difference between qualities that are and are not attainable.

Some students may claim they have no one they look up to or identify as a hero. Ask them to think back to who they thought was pretty cool when they were younger.

Participants may have difficulty seeing the connections between their role models and their own behaviors. You can help them make the connection by focusing, in the discussion, on how a current behavior of one of the group members is similar or different from that of a role model.

MY OBSERVATIONS ▶

_____

_____

_____

_____

_____

_____

_____

_____

_____

_____

44.
Role Model Collage

Recommended
ages: 10 +

Phase 2

GOAL ▶	■ Group members identify characteristics they want in role models.
DESCRIPTION ▶	Group members make collages representing the qualities they want in a role model.
MATERIALS NEEDED ▶	An assortment of magazines that can be cut up, paper, scissors, and glue or tape.
DIRECTIONS ▶	Initiate a discussion of role models. Ask participants whom they look up to or admire. These could be people they know personally or people they have seen or heard about from others or in the media. Ask them to name qualities these people have that they admire. Write the qualities they identify on a chalkboard or newsprint.

Ask group members to look through the magazines and identify pictures that reflect two or three qualities that are important to them. Have them cut out these pictures and make a collage.

Continue to discuss the qualities they admire while they are reviewing the magazines and making their collages. Try to deepen their understanding by asking probing questions about the characteristics that they have identified. For instance, if they identify having a lot of money as an admirable characteristic, you might ask if there is something about the way they use the money that is admirable. Are they generous? Are they careful about how this money is used? When they have completed their collages, have each group member discuss his or her collage and the meaning behind the pictures. Ask if it is realistic for them to attain these qualities.

THINGS TO THINK ABOUT ▶	Some participants try to do the least amount of work possible or try to do the activity as fast as possible to get it over with. Encourage them to take their time in this process.
MY OBSERVATIONS ▶	

45.
Interviewing Someone with Peaceful Behavior Experience

Recommended ages: 10 +

Phase 2

GOALS
- Group members increase their connections with positive role models.
- Group members increase their understanding of options to using violent behavior.

DESCRIPTION
Group members interview people who have behaved in a peaceful manner and share their responses with the group.

MATERIALS NEEDED
One Interview Questions worksheet (page 111) for each participant.

DIRECTIONS
Pass out the Interview Questions worksheets. Tell participants that within the next two weeks they are to find a person who has behaved in a peaceful manner and ask these questions of that person. They are to bring the answers back to the group. Set a time when you want them to return with and review the questions. Tell them they will share the answers given by the person they interviewed. When they have shared the information at the follow-up session, ask them additional questions such as the following:

- Did you already know this person? If so, how long?
- Who is this person?
- What interesting things did you learn from talking with this person?
- Knowing what you do now, what else might you want to ask this person?
- What was it like interviewing this person?
- Were you nervous?
- Was the other person nervous?
- What were some of the similarities in the responses of the people interviewed?

Tell participants that these interviews will be saved for review at the final session.

THINGS TO THINK ABOUT
Have the group members list several people to choose among. Their first choice may not be available. It is helpful to have some contact with each of the group members between sessions to see if they have found someone to interview.

MY OBSERVATIONS

Interview Questions

- What is your name?

- Whom did you look up to when you were my age?

- What good things did they do that you liked?

- Which behaviors of theirs do you try to do also?

- What goes through your mind when you come up against a situation in which you could choose to be violent but you choose to be peaceful instead?

- What helps you decide not to use violence?

- What options come to mind for you in these situations?

- Who are people you turn to for support now?

- How do you get support from others?

- Is there any other piece of information that would be helpful for me?

Thank you for your help. The wisdom you shared with me and your role-modeling will help me in the future.

46.
Reinventing Reputations

Recommended
ages: 10 +

Phase 2

GOALS ▶
- Group members understand what a reputation is.
- Group members understand how reputations affect people.

DESCRIPTION ▶
Group members identify the types of reputations people have, examine how they are acquired, and develop a list of positive reputations.

MATERIALS NEEDED ▶
Circle of Courage talking piece.

DIRECTIONS ▶
Discuss reputations with the group members, noting that a reputation is often a short label used to describe a person or a group. These labels may be neutral, positive, or derogatory. Everybody has reputations, and we may have one reputation with some people and another reputation with other people. We have reputations with family members, employers, teachers, principals, and peers. Even when others don't know us, they find ways of putting us in categories. Sometimes it is by the way we dress, the way we talk, or what we do. Rarely do we escape having people make assumptions about us.

List on the chalkboard or newsprint four current movie stars, four sports figures, and four prominent people in the community. Ask group members to describe these people and write the descriptions under each person's name. Next ask participants if the attributes identified are facts or assumptions. Ask what they are based on.

Ask participants to name reputations that are present within their school or community. List on the chalkboard or newsprint all suggestions that are offered, even if you know that they only describe one or two people. They may include labels such as *jocks* or *burnouts*, or something entirely different. Ask participants questions such as the following:

- What do the people who belong to these groups do?
- What if people thought you were in one of these groups, but you didn't agree?
- What determines whether or not you are in a certain group with a certain reputation?
- Do any of the reputations share similar characteristics?
- Which ones are different?
- Which reputations are preferred?
- Which reputations are more negative?

Next, ask participants to name reputations people have within their families. They may include labels such as *troublemakers, good boys, good girls, active, energetic, difficult, angry, depressed.* List these suggestions on the chalkboard or newsprint. Lead a discussion with questions such as the following:

- How do your family members see you?
- How do different family members see you? (For example, a grandmother may see a different reputation than does a parent or an aunt.)
- Do you have the same reputation among family members and peers? (Probably not. In fact, most participants prefer not to have to discuss with their families what reputations they have at school.)

Next, explain that people tailor their behavior to maintain reputations they want to have. In other words, there are young people who want to appear tough and unapproachable so no one sees them as people who can be taken advantage of or vulnerable to attack. Some young people engage in risky behaviors or act crazy around others in order to make sure people keep their distance. It may seem weird that people would try to keep reputations that often work against them. Lead a discussion with questions such as the following:

- Do you know anyone who maintains a reputation with teachers or other students that works against them?
- How might it work against them? (For example, putting the person in an increasingly isolated place, making the person feel disconnected from friends or adults at school.)
- What options might this person have to alter the reputation?

Have the group members now develop a list of positive reputations. These should reflect ways that they would like to be seen in school. List their suggestions on the chalkboard or newsprint. Have each group member choose at least three of these reputations and state in a Circle of Courage (see page 35) which ones they would like to have for themselves in their school or community. Lead a discussion using questions such as the following:

- Is it possible to change a reputation?
- If not, what are the barriers or obstacles that stand in the way?
- What steps could a person take to change how others view him or her?

Many participants have fun identifying the types of reputations that exist. These reputations generally exist for small, cohesive groups in school or in other settings. Participants can identify these groups. Asking them to label what groups are called sends the message that you are interested in them and their perspectives. You may also encounter some resistance to defining the types of groups that exist in participants' communities, especially schools. Young people frequently are more comfortable identifying reputations within families and friendship groups. Allow some flexibility for descriptions of groups but maintain respectful communication. This will create safe spaces for more people to share their views. Should some participants begin to name-call others in the group or outside of the group, remind them of the rules. Ask how others might feel if they were called names. Discuss alternatives to name-calling and, if possible, discuss some reasons that people use name-calling. Because most young people do not sit down and think about what kind of reputations they have, let alone the messages they send that maintain these reputations, this can be a powerful group processing time.

This activity can be rich in information about how the group members see themselves individually and as a group. The label that they carry for coming to this group might even be a barrier for them.

Group members often have not been aware of the reputations they have with family members. When group members identify how family members and others see them, they may feel empowered to try to change these labels.

MY OBSERVATIONS ▶

_____

_____

_____

_____

_____

_____

_____

_____

_____

47.
Reputations: The Good, the Bad, and the Struggling

Recommended ages: 10 +

Phase 2

GOALS ▶
- Group members increase their understanding of the types of reputations they have acquired.
- Group members identify the prices that they pay for maintaining these reputations.

DESCRIPTION ▶
Participants begin discussion and activities regarding their bullying behaviors, purposes for the behaviors, and possible alternative behaviors.

MATERIALS NEEDED ▶
One My Reputations worksheet (page 117) for each participant and pens or pencils.

DIRECTIONS ▶
Begin with a general discussion about reputations (see Activity 46, Reinventing Reputations). Brainstorm with the group a list of labels placed on people.

Pass out the My Reputations worksheets and ask participants to fill them out. They should begin by listing five significant people in their lives: a parent, a sibling, a friend, a teacher, a grandparent, and so on. You should not ask students to fill in the fourth column unless they are eleven years old or older. When they have completed the chart, lead a discussion using questions such as the following:

- What kinds of people did group members identify in their charts?
- How were these people similar?
- How were they different?
- What were the reputations group members identified? (Again ask about similarities and differences.)
- What rewards did group members say they got from their reputations? (Again ask about similarities and differences.)
- Were there any drawbacks or negative consequences from these reputations? (Again ask about similarities and differences.)

This activity is useful simply to allow participants to discover that with reputations (good or bad) come benefits and limitations. However, make sure that the discussion begins on a general note. Participants will probably tune out very quickly if they believe they are going to get labeled or if there is even a remote chance they will be shamed.

There will be some students who state that they do not fit into any group. Investigate this perspective further. Are they uncomfortable with the reputations around the school? What type of reputation might come as a result of not having a group to fit into?

Some group members may initially say they like the negative reputations they have attained. If they do, discuss what they gain by having these reputations. Let them know you believe these reputations will affect their behavior negatively.

MY
OBSERVATIONS ▶

My Reputations

Significant Person	My Reputation with This Person	Reward I Get from This Reputation	Drawback to This Reputation

48.
Woogie Woogie

GOAL

- Group members can respond to situations in a flexible manner.

DESCRIPTION

The facilitator reads simple statements or situations, and group members act them out silently for short periods of time, one after the other.

MATERIALS NEEDED

Index cards prepared by the facilitator with statements such as the following, which suggest situations to act out:

- You are playing catch with one other person.
- You are in the grocery store trying to decide what food you're going to pick out.
- You are painting a picture of a mountain scene.
- You are playing checkers with another person.
- You are your favorite zoo animal.
- You are the main singer in a rock band.
- You are driving a formula race car.
- You are riding a horse.

DIRECTIONS

Explain to the group that they will learn in this activity to act "as if." Tell them they have entered a space entirely apart from what is outside the doors of the room. They have traveled to a safe space where they may act in ways that they could not act outside. They are free of all previous limitations and expectations. Therefore, they will now be able to "Woogie, Woogie."

Tell them that they may think this activity is stupid or useless. Ask them to let go of this thought. Note that their responses to suggestions during the activity will be observed.

To warm up for this exercise, have group members stand in a circle and turn to their left. Emphasize that this is just a warm-up activity. You as the facilitator will participate in this activity. Participants should do as you do, shuffling their feet quickly in very tiny steps with their hands hanging at their sides and saying, "Woogie, woogie, woogie, woogie, woogie." They will continue doing so until you tell them to turn around and go the opposite direction. This time, they will take giant steps and say, "Ee-oo, ee-oo, ee-oo, ee-oo." Tell them to turn again and repeat the woogie actions, then turn again and repeat the ee-oo actions. Do this several times.

Now explain that you are going to ask them to act "as if." Tell them that people can get stuck in reacting to problematic situations with violence, but this is not acceptable. This part of the activity is to help them identify new and creative ways of doing things. Tell them you will call out statements that you will read from index cards, and they are to act out the situation or statement that you call out. They are not to use any words or sounds. When they have had from thirty seconds to two minutes to act out the card, call out another statement or situation. You should be able to use twenty to thirty situations. You may wish to repeat some that the group members seem to especially enjoy. Encourage the group members to use the time entirely for acting out and staying within the character they have chosen for themselves. After they have completed acting "as if," have the group sit in a circle and ask them questions such as the following:

- Which situations were the most challenging?
- What was challenging about them?
- Which ones were the most fun? Why?

THINGS TO THINK ABOUT ▶

This activity is very valuable in building group cohesion. However, it is especially challenging to get group members to participate in it, and it requires thorough processing at the end of the activity for participants to understand why it is included. It can produce anxiety for participants because it seems so different from what they are used to doing. They may also feel silly or embarrassed. When participants feel anxious, they are apt to resort to past coping skills such as refusing to participate or resisting by making the activity difficult. Be patient and encourage participants to look for what they have to gain in the activity. Also let them know that it is strongly suggested that they participate.

Try not to worry if members who are initially resistant put only minimal energy into the activity. It still allows them to feel part of the group. If there are group members who definitely refuse to participate, see pages 6–7 for information on dealing with resistance.

MY OBSERVATIONS ▶

_____

_____

_____

_____

_____

_____

49.
Music Lyrics and What They Say

GOALS

- Group members better understand the lyrics they listen to in songs.
- Group members are able to identify messages sent through songs.

DESCRIPTION

Group members listen to and read the lyrics of songs from their favorite singers and identify the messages and impacts.

MATERIALS NEEDED

Each group member should provide the lyrics of two songs by his or her favorite singer. This should be done two sessions prior to this activity. Select one song from each participant and make enough copies for each group member.

DIRECTIONS ▶

Review the lyrics of each song with the entire group. After each song, ask questions such as the following:

- What is the basic message of the song?
- Who is the audience for the song?
- What images are in the song?
- What messages are being conveyed about girls and women? About violence? About how boys should treat girls?
- What is the goal of the song?
- How is it supposed to impact the audience?
- Is it supposed to elicit an emotional response?
- What kind of feelings is it supposed to tap?
- Who would you play this song for? Parents? Grandparents? An employer?
- What response might your girlfriend or boyfriend have to this song?
- Might they be offended?
- What might some people find offensive?

If the song contains language that is negative, ask the group to interpret the negative words and phrases. Ask them the purpose for including this language. Have them suggest other ways these same things could be said.

THINGS TO THINK ABOUT ▶

It may be helpful for you to bring in some lyrics from several popular songs. Sometimes group members forget to bring in lyrics.

Some lyrics may be offensive or hurtful. You can eliminate hurtful words from the copy before distributing it. Explain that you will not contribute to the negative messages in this group.

Listen to the lyrics and try to stay objective as you examine them. Judgmental or derogatory comments about the artist can negatively affect your relationship with the group.

MY OBSERVATIONS ▶

_____

_____

_____

_____

_____

_____

_____

_____

_____

_____

_____

_____

_____

50.
Mobile of Peace

GOALS	■ Group members gain enlarged view of the meaning of peace. ■ Group members understand that behaving in a peaceful manner can have positive results. ■ Group members increase their understanding of how their behavior affects others.
DESCRIPTION	Group members create "images of peace" mobiles.
MATERIALS NEEDED	Magazines from which pictures may be cut, scissors, construction paper, glue or tape, yarn or string, and a clothes hanger for each group member.
DIRECTIONS ▶	Explain to the group that they will create individual mobiles of peace. Ask them to cut out images of peace from the magazines. They can glue or tape these images onto their paper, which they have cut into any shape they like, and attach them with string to the clothes hanger. Hang their mobiles from the ceiling in some fashion. As they are cutting out their images, ask questions such as the following: ■ What are you looking for? ■ What catches your eye as being an image of peace? ■ How do you decide if this image fits for your mobile? ■ How do you decide which image to put where? When they have completed their mobiles, have them describe their work, including why they chose to include the images they did. Ask the group to discuss what was shared, using questions such as the following: ■ What sorts of themes did you hear in what was shared? ■ If you could borrow an image from someone else's mobile for your own, which one would you add? ■ Were there images that made you think about peace in a new way? ■ How might your mobile affect others?

While this activity should help group members understand that their images of peace can make a difference for others, do not expect huge insights. This activity may be especially challenging if you are leading it after any kind of public trauma, which can make it difficult for young people to envision or believe in the efficacy of peaceful responses.

_____

_____

_____

_____

_____

_____

_____

_____

_____

_____

_____

_____

_____

_____

_____

PHASE THREE

101

Support Group Activities

For Teenagers Who Bully

A Leader's Manual
for Secondary Educators
and Other Professionals

51.
Defining Violence, Abuse, and Bullying

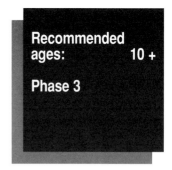

Recommended ages: 10 +

Phase 3

GOAL		■ Group members understand the terms *violence, abuse,* and *bullying.*
DESCRIPTION		Group members brainstorm examples of different kinds of violence and draw "definition spirals."
MATERIALS NEEDED		A piece of paper for each group member and pens or pencils.
DIRECTIONS		

Ask group members for a definition of *violence.* Explain to the group that violence is words and actions that hurt others, whether intentional or accidental.

Draw four columns on a chalkboard or newsprint. Label the columns "Verbal," "Physical," "Emotional," and "Sexual." Ask group members to brainstorm examples of violence. As they name examples, write them under the appropriate column. When there are at least twenty examples in each column, pass out a piece of paper and a pen or pencil to each participant and have them make definition spirals. Ask them to choose one word from a list and write it as small as possible in the middle of the paper. They select and write a second word from the same list so that it begins to wrap around the first word. They then select a third word to continue the spiral and go on in this fashion until all the words in a list are used. This demonstrates that all of the examples are attached in some form. You may wish to have group members create a definition spiral for all four lists.

Lead a discussion, asking questions such as the following:

■ Are there some examples that might fit in more than one list?
■ Are there more ideas you can add to the lists and spirals?
■ Where does the word *bullying* fit best?
■ What types of actions and behaviors could be considered bullying?
■ Are there differences between bullying behaviors and the examples already on the lists?
■ How are others affected by the behaviors?
■ What do other people do when they see bullying behavior?

Explain to group members that, for the purposes of this group, they should understand that *abuse* and *bullying* have the same definition as *violence*: "words or actions that hurt people." Bullying is any behavior that hurts someone else or that intimidates, threatens, or creates fear in the recipient. It is bullying whether the person intended it to be hurtful or not. Explain that group members do not need to agree with this definition, but they do need to understand that this definition is the basis of the work in the group. Ask them what they disagree with or agree with in regard to the definition you presented. Make a note for yourself regarding group members' responses to this definition.

THINGS TO THINK ABOUT ▶

Discussing definitions of *violence, abuse,* or *bullying* can be a touchy subject, especially when group members have been identified as having behaved in violent ways. You can defuse some of the participants' defensiveness by helping them focus on behaviors rather than judgments of people. In addition, you can ask them to begin by focusing on violent behavior that has been directed at them. This should help them be more open to sharing the times and ways in which they have been targeted.

It is helpful to stay concrete in this activity and not to engage in discussions about which type of violent behavior is worse. It helps to establish a common understanding if you approach all types of violence on an equal level.

Many times, students who use violent behaviors feel they are "above the law" because they define their behaviors as necessary to address certain problems. You may be able to help these participants gain a different perspective by focusing on how violent behavior affects others. Helping group members understand the impact bullying or violent behavior has on others is important to establishing a foundation for discussion in future activities. You may not be able to change any minds immediately, but beginning the discussion opens the door to progress in activities that are focused on empathy.

MY OBSERVATIONS ▶

_____

_____

_____

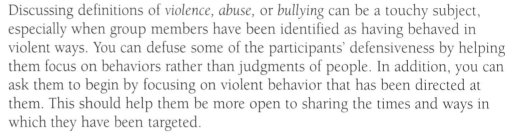

What Is Bullying?

This curriculum is based on the assumption that *bullying* and *abuse* have the same definition as *violence*: "words or actions that hurt people." Bullying is any behavior that hurts someone else or that intimidates, threatens, or creates fear in the recipient. It is bullying whether the person intended it to be hurtful or not.

52.
Recognizing Signals

Recommended
ages: 10 +

Phase 3

GOALS ▶	■ Group members understand the escalation process. ■ Group members learn to identify the signals that they are becoming increasingly tense. ■ Group members learn to disrupt tension before they blow up.
DESCRIPTION ▶	Group members draw the Escalation Cycle, identify a variety of signals that indicate they are getting tense, and write their own signals on their drawing.
MATERIALS NEEDED ▶	Five pieces of newsprint or tagboard posted on the wall, each with one of the following words or phrases: "Body," "Feelings," "Thoughts," "Hot Signal Words," "Hot Signal Situations"; paper for each group member; pencils; and crayons, colored pencils, or markers.
DIRECTIONS ▶	Draw the Escalation Cycle (see page 131) on the chalkboard or newsprint, explain it to group members, and discuss the related issues.

Note for the group that the Escalation Cycle usually is repeated many times in a week or even in a day. For those who have experienced this cycle, it brings on many feelings. Ask the group to share the feelings that a person who is stuck in the cycle might have. (It often ends with feelings of guilt and shame for their behaviors.)

Ask group members to think quietly about what signals they recognize that tell them they are starting to get stressed out. While they are doing this, give them each a piece of paper and ask them to copy the Escalation Cycle figure. Under the words "Build Up" on the chalkboard or newsprint, write: "Body," "Feelings," "Thoughts," "Hot Signal Words," "Hot Signal Situations."

Ask the group members to share what their bodies do when they start getting stressed—when tension starts to build up. List their responses on the large piece of paper labeled "Body." You may need to prompt them with questions such as these: Do your muscles get tight? Do you pace? Does your stomach feel crummy? Do you clench your fists? Do you grind your teeth? Do you get quiet? Do you get loud?

Ask group members to share the feelings they experience. Most will share angry, sad, hopeless, trapped, depressed, confused, frustrated, irritated, annoyed. List these responses on the paper labeled "Feelings."

Next, ask them to share the thoughts that run through their heads when they experience stressful situations, then list these responses on the appropriate paper. These may include thoughts such as: "You can't talk to me that way," "Shut up," "You don't know what you're talking about," "I hate you," "Get out of my face," and "You're stupid."

Next, ask group members to share some of their hot signal words. These are words or phrases that really bother them. Again, list responses on the appropriate paper. These could be names or labels, put-downs, swear words, phrases that demean or threaten their families or friends, and so on.

Finally, ask group members to share hot signal situations. These are places or situations in which they get stressed. List responses on the appropriate paper. These may be family gatherings, school events, discussions of sensitive topics such as grades or friends, riding in the car, being in the dining room, and so on.

Refer back to the left-hand side of the circle labeled "Build Up." Point out that all of the things they have just identified are signals that can alert them that they are getting very tense and need to take care of themselves so they will not "blow up." The sooner they can identify the signals, the better they can take care of themselves.

Have the group members write, in the "Build Up" section of their papers, their own signals as they relate to their bodies, feelings, thoughts, hot signal words, and hot signal situations.

Have the group members then add colors and symbols to this circle.

THINGS TO THINK ABOUT ▶

An understanding of the Escalation Cycle is at the crux of teaching group members alternatives to bullying behaviors. The tools you will be teaching in many other sessions will hinge on participants' ability to recognize their escalation signals. Give this activity plenty of time and monitor the group to find out if they really understand the cycle and the need to intervene for themselves early in difficult situations, not just when the situation is so tense that they are ready to blow up.

You will want to refer to the Escalation Cycle during future sessions when participants are asked to discuss their current situations. Referring to the Escalation Cycle can help them identify when and what they were feeling and thinking, and what their bodies were doing, during a given difficult situation.

It may be difficult for young people to believe that stepping out of the Escalation Cycle requires courage. Help them reframe the idea of bravery, emphasizing the courage it requires to pay attention to their escalation signals and to walk away from a difficult situation rather than fighting it out. Discuss with the group the messages they have received about what they are supposed to do when they get in a jam. Have them talk about the struggles and challenges that exist for someone who wants to walk away from a difficult situation.

MY OBSERVATIONS ▶

Escalation Cycle:
Build Up, Blow Up, Calm Down

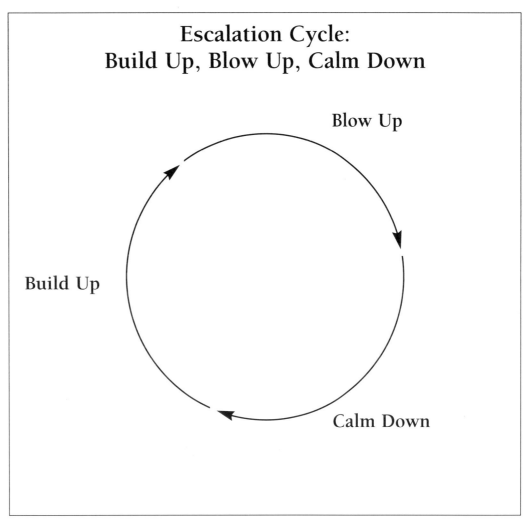

Escalation Cycle: Build Up, Blow Up, Calm Down

The Escalation Cycle is a vicious circle that people get caught in. They can also learn to disrupt the cycle. It has three phases:

1. Build-up phase. The person feels increasing tension.
2. Blow-up phase. The person lashes out and somebody gets hurt.
3. Calm-down phase. After someone has been hurt, the tension is released, but the person feels guilty, ashamed, or embarrassed.

There are many signals during the build-up phase that can alert you to the fact that you are feeling increasingly tense. Paying attention to these signals can help you avoid hurtful behaviors. The earlier you pay attention, the more quickly you can take care of yourself and avoid the blow-up phase.

There are always options to stop the escalation throughout the process. You can choose to step out of the cycle at any point.

It takes courage to stop the cycle. If you are alert, you can recognize your own signals. If you are brave enough, you can take care of yourself and stop the process. Walking away from a situation takes more bravery than fighting it out.

53.
Draw the Anger Volcano

GOALS

■ Group members increase their understanding of their own anger dynamics.
■ Group members increase their understanding of how their anger affects others.

DESCRIPTION

Group members draw a picture that represents their personal anger volcano. Group members then sit in a Circle of Courage to discuss their specific drawings.

MATERIALS NEEDED

Circle of Courage talking piece, paper for each group member, and colored pencils, markers, and crayons.

DIRECTIONS

Have the group discuss volcanoes. Note that they build up heat until they explode or overflow, and the explosion often hurts the people around it. Ask the group how the way in which volcanoes work is similar to the way their anger works. Ask each group member to draw his or her anger as if it were a volcano, paying attention to colors, shapes, and sizes in the pictures. After they have completed their drawings, use the Circle of Courage (see page 35) to have the participants talk about their drawings. Ask for volunteers to talk about their drawings and describe the significance of the colors, shapes, or sizes. Then ask them to describe the feelings they had while drawing the pictures. Continue until all members have had an opportunity to discuss their drawings. Initially, some members may refuse to admit that they are ever angry. Avoid discussing whether or not this is true. Instead, ask questions such as the following:

■ Who has ever been angry?
■ Is there anyone who was angry in the past week?
■ What happened when you got angry?
■ Did you blow up at anyone?
■ Did you see anyone get angry this week?
■ How did this person express his or her anger?

Help the group discuss responses. Sometimes, members may simply call anger something else, such as frustration, confusion, feeling out of control, or rage. Allow a variety of words to be used to refer to anger.

Assist the group members in identifying how they might know when the volcano is going to blow. Use questions such as these:

- What are the signals for you?
- Are there some situations or places where the eruption takes place more often than others?
- Does the anger feel out of control when it is erupting?

You may wish to raise a discussion about the reality of control, noting that people mistake the *feeling* of being out of control for actually being out of control. Even when they are extremely angry, they are still making decisions. These decisions rarely include doing harm of major consequence to somebody. When major physical violence or deaths occur in these situations, they were often not intended. This is a good opportunity for you to emphasize the difference between intention, which often is positive, and the negative impact of behavior.

THINGS TO THINK ABOUT ▶

There are other images besides volcanoes to demonstrate anger. One other example is a thermometer that rises and bursts if it gets too hot. Another metaphor is a balloon that is overfilled with air.

In addition, have group members discuss what happens in the aftermath of a volcanic eruption. What things are destroyed by the fallout? How do things return to normal? How do people who live around the volcano feel? What might be their biggest anxiety, even if they haven't seen an eruption in a long time?

MY OBSERVATIONS ▶

_____

_____

_____

_____

_____

_____

_____

_____

_____

54.
Confusion and Frustration Can Be My Friends

Recommended ages: 10 +

Phase 3

GOALS ▶
- Group members understand that confusion and frustration are precursors to anger.
- Group members are able to manage these feelings.

DESCRIPTION ▶
Group members identify feelings associated with confusion and frustration, act out confusion and frustration in relation to difficult situations, and make posters to communicate their usefulness as signals.

MATERIALS NEEDED ▶
One sheet of newsprint for each group member and pens, pencils, or markers.

DIRECTIONS ▶
Write the terms *confusion* and *frustration* on the chalkboard or newsprint, discuss what they mean, and draw lines down from each of them. Ask the group to share other feelings that grow out of these two feelings. Write these as well.

Present at least three frustrating or confusing situations that might realistically happen in a school or other institutional setting or at home. Have the group members demonstrate the feelings without talking as they relate to these situations. Explain that these feelings are useful signals. Group members should allow themselves to experience these feelings rather than fear them; recognizing confusion and frustration can help them understand what is going on. Have group members list ideas of what these feelings might signal in the situations presented.

Have each participant sketch a rough draft of a poster that will send a message to young people who have difficulty expressing feelings. The message is that they should be aware of their feelings so that they can choose a positive way to express them. Then ask group members to share with each other how elements of their posters convey this message. Ask questions such as the following:

- If you saw this poster, what would you remember?
- Does it have any similarities to the other posters?

THINGS TO THINK ABOUT ▶

MY OBSERVATIONS ▶

The messages on the posters should get the attention of their audience, whether they cause shock, confusion, warm feelings, or some other reaction. However, you may need to monitor the posters to make sure they do not contain swearing, offensive words or images, or meaningless violent images.

If possible, have the posters displayed. If done in a school or other institution, ask staff members to write comments on index cards to the group members. This feedback can be affirming to the participants.

_____

_____

_____

_____

_____

_____

_____

_____

_____

_____

_____

_____

_____

_____

_____

_____

55.
Being Assertive

GOALS

- Group members learn what assertiveness is.
- Group members learn assertive communication skills.
- Group members feel empowered in challenging situations.

DESCRIPTION

Facilitator demonstrates aggressive and passive-aggressive communication techniques, teaches the definition of *aggressive, passive, passive-aggressive,* and *assertive* behavior, and leads discussion on assertiveness guidelines. Group members share times when they have felt listened to.

MATERIALS NEEDED

A copy of Guidelines for Assertive Communication (page 139) for each group member, and a chair (optional).

DIRECTIONS

Ask for a volunteer to stand in the middle of the group circle as you talk about the term *assertiveness.* While speaking, walk closer to the person in the middle until it seems he or she feels uncomfortable with the distance between the two of you. Then have this person sit on the floor or in a chair. Move even closer and raise your voice while asking questions such as these:

- What is your name?
- How old are you?
- Where were you yesterday at 3:30 P.M.?
- Why do you always hang out with that person?

Next, start talking under your breath about this person while you face the other direction. Then turn back to the person and say that you are mad, but laugh while saying it.

Point out that you just demonstrated aggressive and passive-aggressive communication.

Lead a discussion on the definitions of *aggressive, passive, passive-aggressive,* and *assertive behavior* (see "What Is Assertive Behavior?" on page 138).

Pass out the Guidelines for Assertive Communication and lead a discussion on how to use them. Note that using the Guidelines for Assertive Communication can increase group members' chances for getting their points heard by others.

Ask the group to take turns sharing times when they have felt that someone listened to them and actually heard their point. When everyone has had a turn, ask questions such as the following:

- What was happening in these situations?
- How did the other person demonstrate that he or she was listening?
- How did you feel when this person listened to you?
- Did you get what you wanted right away?
- If not, was it helpful for you to know that at least this person listened?

THINGS TO THINK ABOUT ▶

Some members may try to argue that this stuff does not work, that you, the facilitator, must live in a dreamland. Concede for the sake of argument that it may not work, but for this activity they will at least have a chance to try it in the dreamland where you live.

You may also suggest that this focus may be a way to avoid trying new things. Point out that acting aggressively is similar to having a tantrum, that no one would want to be around someone who lay down on the ground and kicked and screamed every time he or she did not get what was wanted, and that people also don't want to be around someone who is violent or aggressive.

You may also challenge group members to come up with situations where assertiveness will not work. You may choose to demonstrate some assertive responses to these situations. Remind group members that the goal of being assertive is to say how you feel and what you want. Once you have done this, you have been successful.

Some group members may say that this type of approach shows that you are a wimp. Ask the members to give you an example of a conflict situation. Ask them to tell you how a wimp might handle that situation. Then help them see the difference between the wimp's reaction (a passive reaction) and an assertive response.

MY OBSERVATIONS ▶

_____

_____

_____

_____

_____

_____

What Is Assertive Behavior?

Aggressive behavior is when you are demanding, are disrespectful, or simply try to take what you want. Aggressive behavior can become violent or abusive. The goal of being aggressive is to get what you want. This aggressive communication style is different than being aggressive in sports. When people act aggressively, they are indirect in expressing their feelings and are usually unclear about what they want.

Passive behavior is when you just go along with what everybody else wants instead of saying what you want or need. Those who predominantly use passive communication appear to be manipulative and to be hiding their feelings. They are rarely direct about what they want. These people have the same goal as the people who are aggressive: to get what they want. This kind of behavior can leave you feeling empty, deprived, and resentful.

Passive-aggressive behavior is when you just go along with what everybody else wants instead of saying what you want or need, but you feel angry or resentful and get back at people later. The way you get back at them isn't necessarily connected to what you're mad about, so it can be pretty confusing to everybody involved.

Assertive behavior is when you say clearly and directly what you want and how you feel but remain respectful of the other person and his or her wishes as well. You may or may not get what you want, but you will be able to feel good about yourself, and you will face less risk of getting hurt or getting into trouble.

Guidelines for Assertive Communication

- Prepare yourself. Ask:
  1. What is my frame of mind?
  2. What is my goal in trying to address this issue?
  3. What is the main thing I want to communicate?
  4. What am I feeling and what do I want to have happen in this situation?

- Use I-statements.

- Use respectful body language.

- Stand or sit at a respectful distance.

- Pay attention to timing. It may be best to address your concerns at another time if the other person is so upset that he or she cannot be open to talking.

- Avoid asking questions.

- If you must ask questions, ask only clarifying questions, like "Could you help me better understand how you are seeing this situation?" or "Would it be helpful for me to try to explain what I'm saying another way?"

- Be aware that it is better to understand than to be understood.

56.
One's Up, One's Down

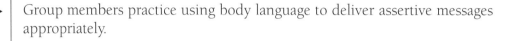

Recommended ages: 10 +

Phase 3

GOALS ▶	■ Group members understand how body position and body language affect communication. ■ Group members increase options for addressing another person in an assertive manner.
DESCRIPTION ▶	Group members practice using body language to deliver assertive messages appropriately.
MATERIALS NEEDED ▶	Chairs or stools for everyone in the group, Circle of Courage talking piece.
DIRECTIONS ▶	Review elements and goals of assertiveness (see "What Is Assertive Behavior?" on page 138). Ask if there are some people with whom it is more difficult to be assertive than others. Ask which adults they can be assertive with. Guide their discussion so that it does not focus on aggressiveness. Discuss appropriate body language, noting that how a message is delivered can make a difference in how it is received. It is important to say assertive words with a body position that is respectful and conveys equality, not superior power or aggression. Examples of confusing body language include: delivering an assertive message but standing uncomfortably close to the other person, or talking to the person with your back toward him or her. As a demonstration for the group, have one group member stand on a chair or a stool and read the following assertive statement to another member: "When you tell other people lies about me, I feel hurt, left out, and like you're trying to get at me. I want you to be direct with me and tell me what's on your mind." Then have the same member step down off the chair and stand face-to-face at a comfortable distance from the other member and read the statement again. Ask the receiver if the two messages felt different. Ask which way he or she would prefer to be addressed. Begin a discussion in a Circle of Courage (see page 35) about a time when the participants felt they were being talked down to. Ask them to describe how the other person could have been assertive with them instead of approaching them in that one-up, one-down position. Have the group brainstorm assertive statements that they could use with a parent, a teacher, or another student.

Next, have participants

1. pair up and practice saying these assertive statements in an equalized position

2. choose one member of the pair to climb onto a chair and practice saying the statements to the other person from a one-up position

3. reverse positions and have the same person give the same message from the one-down position

Lead a discussion asking questions such as the following:

- What did you see happen during the practice?
- How was it similar to what you've seen happen outside this group?
- What would not work in a real-life situation?
- What differences would you see in someone's reactions if they were in a one-down position or a one-up position?

Point out that the group is learning more complicated information about assertive behavior. Affirm them in the progress they have made.

THINGS TO THINK ABOUT ▶

The movement in this activity may prove challenging. Help the members to avoid power struggles in deciding who is in what position initially. You may want to choose who does what first.

Some group members may continue to feel they must exert power by delivering the message with an aggressive body posture. Part of the challenge for you will be to show them how they might come off to others and that aggressive posture does not get them what they really wanted in the beginning.

MY OBSERVATIONS ▶

_____

_____

_____

_____

_____

_____

_____

57.
The Passive Game

GOAL

- Group members increase their understanding of what passive behaviors entail.

DESCRIPTION

Group members do a variety of role plays in which they experience acting passively.

MATERIALS NEEDED

Three pieces of paper for each group member on which instructions are written for actions that a participant can take in class. Examples include the following:

- Tell me how you're feeling right now.
- Raise your right hand.
- Pick up the book.
- Close your eyes.
- Fold your hands.
- Give me a high five.

DIRECTIONS

Begin a discussion about the term *passive* (see "What Is Assertive Behavior?" on page 138). Ask participants questions such as the following:

- Why do people behave passively? (Frequently it is to avoid getting hurt more or put down.)
- What is the ultimate goal of passive behavior? (Getting what you want.)
- What are some examples of passive behavior?
- How do others treat people who behave passively?
- What is an example of a message given by passive behavior? (If I ignore you, maybe you'll stop.)

Ask the group to do some acting. Have them act as if they were watching a concert of their favorite musical group. They should look like they are enjoying themselves and getting really involved in the concert. After thirty seconds, tell them to become passive. They should look like they are taking in the concert without much excitement, are bored, perhaps don't even want to be there.

Next, have them act as if they were spending time with a close friend doing an activity they love to do. Encourage them to act as if it is one of the best times they have ever had. As they are acting this out, ask group members to tell you what it is that they are doing and who they are with. After thirty seconds, call out that they are to switch to passive. Again they should look disinterested in the activity they are pretending to do.

After you have given them several situations to experience the difference between being an engaged participant and a passive participant, ask questions such as the following:

- What feelings did you have when you were pretending to be an active participant?
- What feelings did you have when you were acting in a passive role?
- Which approach takes more energy and more thought?
- How do others see you when you are acting in a passive manner?
- Is this how you want to be seen?
- What feelings lead a person to behave passively?
- What other ways are there to express these feelings besides behaving passively?

Break group members into three-person teams, each team member taking one of the following roles: Passive Actor, Message Giver, and Observer. Hand the Message Giver three pieces of paper, each containing an instruction to give to the Passive Actor. The Passive Actor must continue to respond as much as possible in a passive manner. This may mean ignoring the Message Giver or being very slow in responding. The Message Giver has thirty seconds to get the Passive Actor to complete the actions. The Observer simply watches to see to what lengths the Message Giver goes in trying to get the Passive Actor to follow the instructions. Have team members rotate roles so that everyone gets the chance to be in each role.

After everyone has had a turn in each role, have group members sit in a circle to discuss their experience. Ask questions such as the following:

- What did you feel like as the Message Giver?
- What did you feel like as the Passive Actor?
- What did you feel like as the Observer?
- What thoughts did you have in each of these roles?
- What are the advantages of acting in a passive manner?
- What are the disadvantages of acting in a passive manner?
- What are some of the reasons someone might act in a passive manner? (Fear, confusion, anger, wanting to go along with everyone else and feel included, refusing to be controlled by another person.)
- In what kind of situations might someone act passively if they were having these feelings?
- What information or help could you offer to a friend whom you see acting in a passive manner?
- What are some ways to respond to someone who acts in a passive manner?

  - "You seem pretty stressed, what's going on?"
  - "Is there anyone you can talk to about what you're feeling?"
  - "I'd like to hear what you are thinking and what's going on for you."

THINGS TO THINK ABOUT ▶

Since many of these participants tend to be aggressive, they may struggle to act in a passive manner. Encourage them to follow the rules.

Encourage participants to do the activity even if they say they do not understand the meaning of the term *passive*. They often gain insight as they role-play.

MY OBSERVATIONS ▶

58.
Communicate Assertively

GOALS ▶

- Group members integrate assertiveness into their repertoire of communication skills.
- Group members identify ways to express anger appropriately.

DESCRIPTION ▶

Through the use of role-playing, group members will practice assertive communication.

MATERIALS NEEDED ▶

None.

DIRECTIONS ▶

Explain to group members that to act assertively, they must know at least two things about themselves: their real feelings and what they want. Have them say these things clearly.

Draw four columns on a chalkboard or newsprint. Label them "Situation," "Details," "Feelings," and "Benefits of Assertiveness." Brainstorm and list in the first column situations that have triggered anger for group members. In the second column, identify what happened and all people involved in the situation. Have group members identify additional feelings associated with these situations and list them in the third column. In the fourth column, write some benefits to using assertive behavior. Some examples are: it reduces the risk of getting into trouble; people see you as responsible; you get respect; others will trust you more.

Present this assertiveness model:

I feel _____

when you _____

In this situation I want _____

You may also wish to review the definition of assertiveness (see "What Is Assertive Behavior?" on page 138).

Have participants take turns role-playing with you the identified situations using the assertiveness model. Emphasize to the group that they should find ways of being assertive using their own words. This will make role plays more real to them. Apply the model to as many situations on the list as possible. You may wish to begin, in the role plays, as the person who is upset and needs to be assertive. This will allow you to demonstrate how the process works and the accompanying rewards. You may then switch to the receiving role in the role plays. As group members begin to appear comfortable with the assertiveness model and with others in the group, you may want to have them role-play with each other. Certainly there are cautions that go along with role-playing with participants; however, as you observe the group members, you will be able to judge whether participants are ready to do the role plays by themselves.

Discuss some of the possible challenges and struggles that may occur for participants the next time they try to act in an assertive manner. Begin the discussion by noting that the primary goal of aggressive behavior or passive behavior is to get what you want, while the goal of assertive behavior is to express your feelings and desires. Use questions such as the following in your discussion:

- How might people respond if you say how you feel?
- If they say they don't care, how do you stay assertive?
- What kind of reputation might you get if you share your feelings?
- In what ways does being assertive show your courage?

THINGS TO THINK ABOUT ▶

These role plays can be fun for the facilitator and participants, but you may need to remind group members numerous times to approach situations with the goal of saying how they feel and what they want. It is important for group members to make the connection between assertiveness and having success. It is also important to discuss and define success: presenting themselves in an appropriate manner and avoiding violence. Point out that they may not get what they want, but getting what one wants immediately is really the primary goal for those who tend to behave aggressively or passively. Being satisfied with presenting oneself in a nonviolent, appropriate manner is a cognitive learning step for group members.

It may be helpful for you to also role-play disrespectful communication, although you do not need to be aggressive in this. Simply find ways to express reactions that might pose a challenge to the group members as they try to act in an assertive manner. Try to provide examples of respectful behavior even when not being assertive. Much of the outcome of the role plays will be guided by your participation.

Often, group members are looking for ways to stump the facilitator. However, if you remain objective during the role play, assertive responses will almost always be the most beneficial and appropriate ways to address the situation, no matter how terrible the situation is.

MY OBSERVATIONS ▶

59.
When I'm Angry

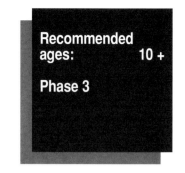

Recommended
ages: 10 +

Phase 3

GOALS ▶	■ Group members integrate assertiveness into their repertoire of communication skills. ■ Group members have a better understanding of how to make assertive behavior choices when their emotions are escalating. ■ Group members integrate nonviolent responses in problematic situations.
DESCRIPTION ▶	Group members identify a situation in which they have felt angry or frustrated and role-play assertive communication.
MATERIALS NEEDED ▶	None.
DIRECTIONS ▶	Ask group members to share situations in which they have gotten angry, frustrated, or confused and ended up in some kind of fight or struggle. Write these situations on the chalkboard or newsprint. Taking each situation in turn, ask the participant who described the situation these questions:

■ What were you thinking that led to your feeling of anger or frustration?
■ What did you intend to communicate to the person(s) you were angry with?
■ Exactly what did you say?

Next, ask the group:

■ What message did you hear in the words said by the participant?

When you have repeated this process for several situations, ask the group:

■ What makes communicating in a clear way so difficult when you are angry?
■ What conclusions are people apt to jump to when they are angry? (You are accusing me of something, and so on.)

You may wish to review the definition of assertive behavior outlined on page 138. Here are some thoughts to share before you go on to the main body of the activity.

It can be difficult to act assertively if you are used to acting aggressively. People tend to return to old behaviors because they are comfortable. Using assertive behaviors may feel awkward or weird at first. In addition, others may challenge you and suggest that you are acting out of the ordinary. You will probably have to use assertive behavior many times before it feels comfortable.

Being assertive when you're angry can be very challenging. Few adults have mastered these techniques, but they are worth practicing. You feel good about how you handle a situation when you act assertively, and you stay out of trouble.

Ask participants to take turns practicing the following model using the situations they identified at the beginning of the session. You may wish to write the model on the chalkboard or newsprint.

Assertiveness Model
1. Ask to talk.
2. Say something positive.
3. State your concern.
4. Say how you feel and what you want.
5. Ask the other person if he or she understands.
6. Thank him or her for hearing you out.

Ask the students to break into pairs. Have the pairs take turns role-playing for the group the assertive communication model for the situations identified earlier. You may wish to participate in the first role play in order to model for the group how this process can work.

After each role play, ask participants questions such as the following:

- What did you notice about how the process worked?
- How real was the situation for you?
- What was the hardest part?

THINGS TO THINK ABOUT

Some participants may want to act out negative ways of dealing with situations. You may need to discuss with the group the tendency to react with anger and defensiveness even in role-playing situations. Remind participants that this group is meant to focus on positive changes and alternatives, and guide them in doing so.

MY OBSERVATIONS

60.
When Someone Is Angry at Me

GOALS ▶
- Group members are able to develop strategies that promote peaceful and assertive responses to potentially difficult situations.
- Group members increase their use of appropriate behaviors in response to someone else's anger.
- Group members increase their chances of being listened to by a person who is angry.

DESCRIPTION ▶
Group members role-play assertive communication in situations in which someone has been angry at them.

MATERIALS NEEDED ▶
A copy of Assertive Communication: The Listening Side (page 151) for each group member.

DIRECTIONS ▶
Ask the group to share situations in which others have been angry at them. These could be situations in which the participants did or did not do something that provoked the anger. Write the situations on a chalkboard or newsprint. Then lead a discussion, asking questions such as the following:

- How did you respond in these situations?
- How were these situations resolved?
- How do you feel about these people right now?
- How did it feel to be on the other side of anger?
- Does it matter who it is that is mad at us?
- Does it feel different when your mom is mad at you than if a teacher is mad at you?
- Are there places or situations in which the stress would be increased if someone were angry with you?

Explain that assertive behavior can be used when someone is angry with us. This lowers the chance that the situation will become explosive and will get us in trouble. Go over the steps in Assertive Communication: The Listening Side (you may wish to copy these on the chalkboard or newsprint).

Break the group into pairs and have them take turns role-playing for the group the situations identified earlier. Explain that this is a complicated process that takes a lot of practice. Emphasize that no process will guarantee that they will get what they want. However, using this approach helps them get through the situation in a way that preserves their self-respect and keeps them out of trouble. This helps them get what they want in the long run.

After each role play, lead a discussion asking questions such as the following:

- What was the easy part of this role play?
- What are the challenges to handling a situation like this?
- What is unrealistic about this role play and this process?

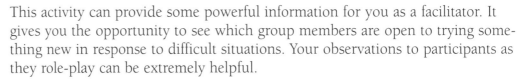

THINGS TO THINK ABOUT ▶

This activity can provide some powerful information for you as a facilitator. It gives you the opportunity to see which group members are open to trying something new in response to difficult situations. Your observations to participants as they role-play can be extremely helpful.

Often group members want to first role-play the negative behaviors, or what they say might "really" happen. Accept their verbal observations and listen to their experiences. However, avoid recreating negative behaviors. The role plays should concentrate on practicing positive responses.

Participation in this activity tends to increase as your presentation to the group is practiced and presented in an enthusiastic and interesting manner. If group members insist that these responses are not realistic, you can say, "You're right, but today and for the purposes of this activity, we will be using them." Some may also say, "I already do that. I know how." Let them know that their experience will be extremely helpful to the other group members and they can show how it should really be done. Maintain a genuinely interested tone in your voice.

MY OBSERVATIONS ▶

_____

_____

_____

_____

_____

_____

_____

Assertive Communication: The Listening Side

Listening well when someone is angry with us and responding with respect, directness, and honesty is also part of assertive communication. These are the steps:

1. Listen to what the person is saying.

2. Listen for how he or she feels and what impact your behavior had on that person.

3. If there are things you don't understand, ask for clarification ("It would be helpful for me to know if this is what you are saying . . .).

4. When it is true, say clearly that you understand.

5. Ask what it is that the other person would like you to do at this time.

6. Say whether or not you are willing to do as he or she requests.

7. Ask if you can share how you see the situation.

8. If given permission, say how you are feeling and what you want.

9. If not given permission, ask if you can schedule a time in the near future when you can let this person know what your perspective is.

10. Ask if this person understands what you just shared.

11. Restate what you are willing to do or change.

12. Thank the person, if you can, for his or her willingness to talk about this.

61.
What Is Respect Like?

Recommended
ages: 10 +

Phase 3

GOAL ▪ Group members understand what respectful behavior is.

DESCRIPTION ▶ Group members imagine how respect, violence, and peace look, sound, feel, taste, and smell.

MATERIALS NEEDED ▶ One Respect worksheet (page 153) for each participant and pencils.

DIRECTIONS ▶ Explain to group members that most of us have five senses: sight, hearing, touch, taste, and smell. Hand out the worksheets and ask each group member to complete the sentences. After all group members have completed their sentences, ask them to read some of their sentences. List them on the chalkboard or newsprint. Ask questions such as the following:

▪ What do you notice about these lists?
▪ What are the similarities?

Have each group member choose one of the sentences he or she wrote and draw a picture of the statement. After all group members have completed their pictures, ask them to describe their pictures, explaining what was included, what was not included, what colors were used, and so on.

THINGS TO THINK ABOUT Have group members complete the sentences with as little thought as possible. Too much thinking can get in the way of a meaningful response.

Having them connect with their senses increases their understanding of and reinforces the concept. Senses transmit data to the brain; senses also help people to access memory. Associating the concepts with senses will help to establish the memory.

MY OBSERVATIONS

Respect

Respect looks like _____

    sounds like _____

    feels like _____

    tastes like _____

    smells like _____

Violence looks like _____

    sounds like _____

    feels like _____

    tastes like _____

    smells like _____

Peace looks like _____

    sounds like _____

    feels like _____

    tastes like _____

    smells like _____

62.
Telling When Assertiveness Worked

GOALS ▶	■ Group members understand assertive behavior.

- Group members understand assertive behavior.
- Group members increase options for acting in an assertive manner in problematic situations.
- Group members integrate use of assertive behaviors.

DESCRIPTION ▶ Group members identify times when assertive behaviors have been or could have been effective, examine the thoughts and feelings behind the assertive behavior, and play a game that allows them to practice the behaviors.

MATERIALS NEEDED ▶ Circle of Courage talking piece.

DIRECTIONS ▶ **Part 1:** Ask group members to review the definition of *assertiveness* and ask them to share examples of assertive behavior (see "What Is Assertive Behavior?" on page 138). Next, within a Circle of Courage (see page 35), have participants describe problematic situations they have experienced that involved another person. When all participants have shared their stories, go around the circle again. Ask for a volunteer or select a group member (Participant One) whose story will be responded to first. Ask participants to share one way they would be assertive in addressing Participant One's problematic situation. Then ask Participant One if he or she heard suggestions from the group that he or she actually used in responding to the situation or that might have worked well. Write these on the chalkboard or newsprint.

Then put three columns on the chalkboard or newsprint labeled "Feelings," "Thoughts," and "Barriers." Ask Participant One what thoughts and feelings he or she experienced while being assertive and write them on the chalkboard or newsprint. If Participant One did not actually use an assertive behavior but identified instead a behavior that he or she thought would have worked well, ask the participant to identify thoughts and feelings that he or she imagines would have accompanied the behavior. Ask the participant to identify the barriers to using the assertive behavior.

Repeat this process for each group member. Continually emphasize that the behaviors that came out of (or would have come out of) a problematic situation could have made things worse but were instead positive, that the participant chose to do it differently, and that these are examples of tools they already use or can use to address situations and people in an assertive manner. Note that they can develop these tools even further.

Part 2: Go around the circle again, asking each group member to describe a problematic situation they may face in the future, either with an adult or with a peer. As soon as one member has described a situation, have the other members take turns sharing one positive piece of self-talk for that situation. Then ask the member who identified the future situation to share the feelings he or she would expect to have. Finally, go around the circle again, asking group members to suggest assertive responses for the situation. List these as they are identified. Repeat the process for each group member.

Part 3: Write three situations on the chalkboard or newsprint. Write a large number 1, 2, or 3 next to the situations. Read them aloud to the group or ask for a volunteer to read them aloud. Have the group stand up. Stand in the middle of the group. Explain to the group that you are going to face one of them and call out a situation number. The person you are facing is to respond as quickly as possible, either describing an assertive response for the situation or demonstrating the response. Face the participants in random order. You may even wish to face a participant twice in a row. The fun of this exercise is in seeing how quickly they can respond in an assertive manner.

End the activity when everyone has had at least a couple of opportunities to answer in an assertive manner. Lead a discussion using questions such as the following:

- What was the most difficult part about responding?
- What did you think about in order to prepare to act assertively?
- How did you begin to increase your speed in responding in a positive manner?
- What supports are present in the group that might not be there in real life?
- What can you think about to help you act assertively if these supportive people are not around you?

THINGS TO THINK ABOUT ▶ Group members may have difficulty focusing on assertive types of responses. Assist them in developing each list. Revisiting this issue will help them integrate the concepts and processes cognitively, which increases the chance that they will use some of the information.

Try not to feel too defeated or frustrated if they do not seem to understand the assertive approach or do not believe that it is a viable option. Once they begin using the options in the group (whether they like it or not), assertive behaviors will become tools they can choose in future situations.

Some participants need guidance and encouragement during Part 3 to ensure that their reaction is as quick as any other reaction. It may help to frame the activity as a game show. You can provide small rewards to those who answer positively within a certain amount of time.

Because this activity is fairly long, it may be helpful to spread it out over the course of two or more sessions.

MY OBSERVATIONS ▶

You also may want to do this activity over several sessions in order to track the number of assertive responses the group comes up with in a certain amount of time. This way they can visually see how much they are improving. This increases motivation.

_____

_____

_____

_____

_____

_____

_____

_____

_____

_____

_____

_____

_____

_____

_____

_____

_____

_____

_____

63.
Assertive Choices

| **GOALS** ▶ | ■ Group members understand how to act in an assertive manner. |
| | ■ Group members learn and practice assertiveness tools. |

DESCRIPTION ▶ Group members brainstorm ways for fictional characters to use assertive behavior to handle difficult situations. They give examples of their own use of assertive behavior.

MATERIALS NEEDED ▶ None.

DIRECTIONS ▶ Lead a discussion on assertiveness, noting that being assertive is saying clearly, directly, and respectfully how you feel and what you want. However, you cannot control whether you get what you want (see "What Is Assertive Behavior?" on page 138).

Ask participants for an example of a time when they were assertive in their communication during the last week. Ask them to describe the situation in some detail. Have them focus on the thoughts and feelings they had when the problematic situation occurred. Write their contributions on the chalkboard or newsprint. When all group members have related some experience, ask them how they decided to use assertive rather than hurtful behaviors in these situations.

Create a story with the group that describes a young person who has used hurtful behaviors with others. Set a scene and describe some of these behaviors. Then ask the participants to name this fictional character. Write the name on the chalkboard. Draw three columns under the name, labeled "Thoughts," "Feelings," "Actions." Ask the group to brainstorm thoughts that the fictional character may be having in the scene that you have set. Then, write these thoughts in the first column. You may wish to prompt them by asking, "If this person were in a new situation where someone was annoying him (or her), what might he (or she) start thinking?" In the next column, write participants' ideas about the feelings that these thoughts would lead to. In the last column, write group members' ideas of what they think this character would do in the scene.

Next, write the fictional character's name again, draw three columns, and label them in the same way. This time, ask the group to focus especially on getting out of the situation in a safe and nonhurtful manner. Ask participants how the character might change his or her thoughts, leading to more appropriate, assertive responses. Write these in the column labeled "Thoughts." Repeat this process for the "Feelings" and "Actions" columns.

Examples of thoughts may include the following: "I don't need to get involved in this," "I don't need to get into more trouble," "I'm not going to be the problem here." Examples of feelings may include frustrated, angry, hurt, fearful. Examples of actions may include walking away or using an I-statement to say that he or she felt angry.

Once all of these choices have been listed, ask for two volunteers, who will use these situations as a basis for role plays. If the two who role-play appear to be stuck, ask the rest of the group to assist by sharing some of the ideas that were recorded on the chalkboard. After two or three role plays are completed, lead a discussion about assertive behavior by asking questions such as the following:

- How did the role-players demonstrate assertiveness?
- In what situations could you use this assertive approach?
- Whom can you use this assertive approach with?
- Are there situations in which you could not use this assertive approach?
- What are they? (For example, when a participant does not feel safe with another person.)
- Are there people with whom you could not use this assertive approach?
- Who are they? (For example, a teacher the participant has not gotten along with in the past.)
- What would prevent you from being assertive with these people?

THINGS TO THINK ABOUT

Often, group members feel they have to respond with the same violent or aggressive behaviors they have used in the past. Allow yourself the opportunity to jump in and reexplain assertiveness.

Some young people believe that using an assertive approach is for weak people. They have difficulty grasping how people can maintain power and control over a situation. Explain the goal—to say what you want and how you feel—again and again in different words and in a positive, energetic manner. It can be helpful to acknowledge that using an assertive approach can be more difficult than using old behaviors, and using assertive behaviors can feel awkward, especially in the beginning.

MY OBSERVATIONS ▶

_____

_____

_____

_____

_____

64.
Communication with Peers

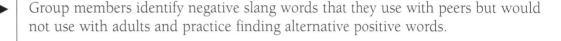

Recommended
ages: 10 +

Phase 3

GOALS ▶	■ Group members understand how they communicate with peers.
	■ Group members increase their ability to communicate positively.
DESCRIPTION ▶	Group members identify negative slang words that they use with peers but would not use with adults and practice finding alternative positive words.
MATERIALS NEEDED ▶	None.
DIRECTIONS ▶	Ask group members to sit in a circle and begin a discussion about how they talk with their peers. Explain that most of us make choices when we talk to someone. Ask participants what words they use with their friends that they do not use with their parents or other adults. Ask why they do not use these words with adults. Point out that their choice of words tells a great deal about who they are.

Point out that they are judged by others, that this is simply a reality even if we do not like it, and that how they talk is one of the ways they are judged. For example, some elderly people fear teenagers because of what they have heard on television or what they have experienced. What your group members say to elderly people like these will either confirm or contradict these beliefs. Some participants, at this point, say they don't care what others say or think about them. Avoid arguing. However, you may wish to ask them if they care what their mothers think of them or if they change how they talk around their mothers.

Have the group list words they use with their peers but not with adults and write them on the chalkboard or newsprint. Ask group members to come up with alternatives that adults can understand. Have them discuss why they use the slang terms.

Next, have participants briefly describe a situation using negative terms. Then have them translate the situation into more positive terms. Have the group members discuss the contrasts between the two. Ask questions such as the following:

■ Which way of talking would be easier?
■ Which way of talking is more difficult?
■ What influences your decision on how you are going to talk?
■ Are there other alternatives?

Now, have group members pair up. Tell one member of each pair to ask for something in a way he or she would communicate with a peer. Have the other person write down what he or she thinks is being asked for. Then ask if everyone understood what they were being asked for. Explain that, even with peers, we develop certain codes and ways of communicating that other peers may not understand.

Have the group discuss what they observed using questions such as the following:

- What do you think about how others view you from the way you act or talk?
- They may reply that they don't care. If so, ask, does anyone you know care about how you act or talk? (Perhaps parents, teachers, and so on.)
- What are these people concerned about?

THINGS TO THINK ABOUT ▶

Sometimes group members do not want to share information about their language. They may see this as an invasion. Rely on your relationship with them and guide the discussion, reminding them that sometimes their language confuses you.

Let the participants know that being an adult sometimes puts you in a place that makes it hard to understand young people in general. This designates the group members as the experts and can have a positive effect on the group process.

Make sure you acknowledge their input and participation whenever possible. This lets them know you are listening and that you do care about them and their views.

Avoid making your own interpretations of what they say. Let them inform you. If you question their perspectives, do it in such a way that you are asking for clarification.

MY OBSERVATIONS ▶

_____

_____

_____

_____

_____

_____

_____

_____

65.
Communication with Adults and Authorities

Recommended ages: 10 +

Phase 3

GOALS ▶
- Group members understand that they choose to communicate differently with different adults.
- Group members increase their ability to communicate appropriately with adults.

DESCRIPTION ▶
Group members identify examples of the differences in their own communication with different adults in their lives.

MATERIALS NEEDED ▶
None.

DIRECTIONS ▶
This activity is similar to Activity 64, Communication with Peers.

Discuss the fact that everyone chooses to communicate differently with different people depending on the relationships they have with them. Young people will communicate differently with other young people than they do with adults, and differently with various adults depending on the adult's age, authority, relationship to the young person, and so on. You may wish to begin the discussion by asking group members to identify specific phrases they use to communicate with adults.

Write at the top of the left side of a chalkboard or newsprint, "School Principal," and at the top of the right side, "Grandparent." Ask participants how they might communicate with each of these people. Some examples might include these: "I only talk to the principal if I have to"; "I ask my grandparent to do things with me." Ask the group to share examples of what they would talk about with each of these people and the kinds of words or phrases they would use. Write their responses in the appropriate column.

Repeat this process with two more adults who the participants come in contact with.

When you have done the process at least twice, ask questions such as the following:

- What do you notice about the different ways that you talk to different adults?
- Do you make a conscious choice to do this?
- How do you make the choice?
- Why do you do this?
- Is it useful?

THINGS TO THINK ABOUT ▶

Participants may find this a strange exercise since it is not something they are apt to think about much. They may even feel it is pointless. However, motivation to participate often increases as they begin to see the differences written out on the chalkboard.

Help the participants be specific in their examples and encourage them to think about the reputation they may have or wish to have with the adults they are discussing.

MY OBSERVATIONS ▶

_____

_____

_____

_____

_____

_____

_____

_____

_____

_____

_____

_____

_____

_____

_____

66.
Obstacle Course of Assertiveness

GOALS ▶

- Group members increase their understanding of *assertiveness*.
- Group members develop assertiveness skills.

DESCRIPTION ▶

Group members select index cards on which are written challenging situations, and they make assertive responses.

MATERIALS NEEDED ▶

Three chairs, each holding as many index cards as there are group members plus one. Each index card should contain one situation. Examples of situations may include the following:

- A student talks to you in class, and the teacher gives you each an hour of detention.
- A student you have teased in the past is at a locker that is next to yours.
- A teacher begins to yell at you for throwing paper in class when you did not do it.
- Another student intentionally bumps into you in the hall.
- You see another student at the mall who you've heard is out to get you.
- There is a person on your sports team who keeps making fun of you.
- When you are at a friend's birthday party at the roller-skating rink, two other youths you don't know push you from behind.

DIRECTIONS ▶

Place the three chairs with their piles of index cards in the middle of the room. Demonstrate this exercise for the group. Go from chair to chair, selecting the top index card from the pile, reading it aloud, and making an assertive statement responding to the situation on the index card. Then, have each group member take a turn doing the same thing. All the other group members will watch the person who is going through the course. If a group member has trouble thinking of an assertive option, have the rest of the group help by brainstorming some responses. Before moving on, the group member doing the course needs to state the assertive option chosen for that situation. Once everyone has gone through the process and has a familiarity of the exercise, gather the cards and shuffle them. Place the cards in stacks on the chairs again. Each participant will repeat the exercise, this time responding as quickly as he or she can. You will time them. If they blurt out a nonassertive response, they lose two points. If they make an assertive response, they get three points. Add the scores at the end.

When they have completed this activity, ask questions such as the following:

- What went through your mind as you were trying to be assertive?
- What were the most difficult situations?
- What were some of the things that got in the way of being assertive?
- Are there any responses you would change?
- If so, how?

THINGS TO THINK ABOUT ▶

The first round of this activity is meant to give participants practice in understanding what their responses should be. It matters little if they get the same situations both times they go through the course. The point is to practice using assertive responses.

It may be helpful to add some challenge to the course by putting the chairs in different parts of the room. Group members might also have fun if other tables or chairs are in their path.

If their first response in a situation is not assertive, find a part of it that may be partially assertive and add to it. Have them repeat the full assertive response.

MY OBSERVATIONS ▶

_____

_____

_____

_____

_____

_____

_____

_____

_____

_____

_____

_____

67.
No One Understands This Part of Me . . .

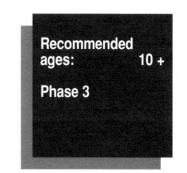

Recommended ages: 10 +

Phase 3

GOALS ▶	■ Group members better understand ways to communicate about themselves.
	■ Group members increase their options for expressing thoughts and feelings.
DESCRIPTION ▶	Group members privately imagine a conversation they have with a trusted person, in which they share things about themselves that they feel no one understands. They then share with others what the person told them.
MATERIALS NEEDED ▶	None.
DIRECTIONS ▶	Ask group members to talk about people to whom they can express their concerns, hopes, thoughts, and feelings, no matter what they are. If they do not have anybody they can share these things with, ask them to think about the qualities such a person would have. Ask them to tell what those qualities are, then list them on the chalkboard or newsprint. Ask the group if they know anyone who reflects all of these qualities. Undoubtedly they will respond in the negative.

Next, ask them to choose three qualities that they would want in a person to whom they were going to tell private things about themselves. Have the group members imagine that this person is in the room with them right now. This person is willing and able to listen to whatever parts of themselves they want to share. Have them imagine telling this trusted friend about parts of themselves that no one else has ever understood. This could be anything from certain activities that they like to a certain style of functioning, such as using procrastination. They are not to share these vulnerable pieces of information with the rest of the group. Have them also imagine this person responding to their request for support.

When they have had time to imagine this conversation with a trusted person, ask them to go around the group and tell what their friend said to them. Then ask questions such as the following:

■ Who was the person you thought of?
■ Is this a real person?
■ Have you thought of this person before?
■ Have you talked to this person before?
■ What was your experience of doing this activity like?
■ What was the most difficult part of this activity?
■ What did you tell yourself to get past the difficult part?
■ Having heard what others' friends might have said, what else might your friend have said to you?

This is a potentially vulnerable position for group members to place themselves in. They may initially respond to this activity with resistance. They may be confused about the purpose behind the activity. The activity is more abstract; however, the discussion that follows makes it more concrete.

Be careful that group members don't reveal the personal information in the group discussion. Let them know that they only need to respond to the statements that they are comfortable with.

Another way to conduct this activity is to use the Circle of Courage (see page 35).

MY OBSERVATIONS ▶

_____

_____

_____

_____

_____

_____

_____

_____

_____

_____

_____

_____

_____

_____

_____

_____

_____

68.
Role-play Appropriate Communication

GOAL ▶ ■ Group members increase their ability to use assertive communication behavior.

DESCRIPTION ▶ Group members identify, within a time limit, whether responses to difficult situations are appropriate or inappropriate.

MATERIALS NEEDED ▶ Several slips of paper for each group member and pencils or pens.

DIRECTIONS ▶ Review the assertive communication processes, asking group members to discuss the goals of assertiveness and how using assertive techniques can feel good as well as result in more positive outcomes (see "What Is Assertive Behavior?" on page 138).

Write "Appropriate Responses" and "Inappropriate Responses" at the top of a chalkboard or newsprint, and pass out several slips of paper to each group member. Ask the group members to verbally describe difficult situations that they have experienced in their school, another institution, or their community and appropriate and inappropriate responses to them. Write their examples under their respective headings on the chalkboard. At the same time, ask the participant who offered the example to write the situation and responses to it on a slip of paper. When each group member has contributed at least one response, collect the papers and pile them in the middle of the group.

Group members will then take turns listening to you read the situations and responses that you have selected from the pile and identifying as many as they can within fifteen seconds as either appropriate or inappropriate. When all the papers have been read, start again until everyone has had two turns.

After the group members have had a chance to do this activity at least twice, ask questions such as the following:

■ What made it difficult to respond correctly?
■ What situations and responses seemed easier to get right?
■ Are there situations when a type of communication is neither appropriate nor inappropriate?
■ Who determines what is appropriate or not in any given situation?
■ Who gets to decide if something was hurtful or not?

In summary, explain to group members that this practice can help them achieve the main goals of using assertive behavior: getting their points across in a constructive way. Getting what they want is never guaranteed, but responding in a positive manner, rather than expecting the other person or the situation to change, is something to feel good about.

THINGS TO THINK ABOUT ▶

You may want to build motivation by increasing competition. You could have two teams compete against each other. You could also invent a number for them to compete against. For instance, you could say, "My last group held the record for the most correct identifications. They were able to make forty correct identifications within two minutes."

Having this activity be faster paced can keep up the group motivation. However, be aware that if it takes longer to explain the directions of the activity than to do it, you may lose group members in the process.

MY OBSERVATIONS ▶

_____

_____

_____

_____

_____

_____

_____

_____

_____

_____

_____

69.
Being Heard by Others

GOALS ▶
- Group members understand how to tell if they are being heard.
- Group members understand how to listen closely to others.

DESCRIPTION ▶
Group members discuss what it means to be really heard and identify people by whom they have felt heard.

MATERIALS NEEDED ▶
Paper for each group member and pencils or pens.

DIRECTIONS ▶
Begin a discussion with the group members about the phrase *being heard*, using questions such as the following:

- What does *being heard* mean to you?
- What is the difference between being heard and being listened to?
- Can you share a specific example of a time when you have felt heard? (Begin a list on the chalkboard or newsprint of people in group members' lives who really hear what they have to say and who acknowledge that their viewpoint has some value.)
- How do you know these people?
- What sets these people apart? (Perhaps it is a school counselor who is trained in these skills, or a lunchroom monitor who simply seems to give some positive attention when necessary.)

Ask group members to brainstorm ways to tell if other people are hearing them. These might include actions taken by the other people such as maintaining eye contact, nodding, giving verbal acknowledgment of their statements, or repeating what was said in their own words.

Ask them to brainstorm ways to find out if they are being heard. These might include the following:

- Ask if the other person understands.
- Ask the other person to repeat what you just said.
- Ask the other person what their opinion is about what you just said.

Have the group identify times when they tend not to listen. These might include when a parent tells them to do a chore, when they are watching a video, when they are in certain classes, or when they don't like a certain teacher. Begin a discussion about why listening is sometimes difficult, asking questions such as the following:

- Are you bored?
- Is the subject matter not interesting?
- Doesn't it apply to you?
- Do you dislike the person who is talking?
- Has the person said something offensive to you in the past?
- Are you preoccupied with something?
- Were you involved in a negative situation with this person?

Begin a discussion about what motivates them to listen and to hear, asking questions such as the following:

- What catches your attention when someone is talking?
- What triggers you to really hear what is being said?
- Does it have to do with respecting the person who is talking?
- Is it when a specific topic interests you?
- Is it when the person being discussed is someone you know?
- Is it when the topic is exciting and fun to think about?

Give group members pieces of paper and ask them to make the following lists:

- Subjects that interest them.
- People in their lives whom they respect and whom they really listen to.
- People with whom they have shared their life story or significant events in their lives.

Ask group members to share parts of their lists. Then continue the discussion with questions such as the following:

- What has been your experience with being heard?
- How would you like it to change?
- Are there some people who do not really hear you that you wish would?
- What makes it difficult to find out if another person hears what you're saying?
- Are there some people who are easier to ask to listen to you than others?
- In what ways can you reduce the barriers to being heard?
- What is the major difference between knowing you're being heard and actively listening to someone?

THINGS TO THINK ABOUT ▶

Having group members identify within the same activity both what it feels like to be heard and how they do or do not listen to others allows them to understand both components of a conversation.

Bullying behaviors often are a reflection of isolation, of not feeling known, included, or acknowledged as an individual. The way persons who bully think and feel in certain situations prompts them to choose self-defeating mechanisms, or bullying behaviors, to address their feelings. Often, group members do not see the connection between not feeling heard and their use of bullying behaviors. Point out this connection. If they have the experience of "being heard," it increases the chance that they will ask assertively for this in the future rather than use bullying behaviors.

MY OBSERVATIONS ▶

_____

_____

_____

_____

_____

_____

_____

_____

_____

_____

_____

_____

70.
Draw the First Problem Situation You Were In

Recommended
ages: 10 +

Phase 3

GOAL ▶

- Group members can reflect on behaviors that got them into trouble.

DESCRIPTION ▶

Group members make drawings of situations when they received consequences for inappropriate behavior and of the thoughts and feelings they had during the situations.

MATERIALS NEEDED ▶

Paper, pencils, and crayons, colored pencils, or markers.

DIRECTIONS ▶

Ask group members to think about one of the first times they received consequences for inappropriate behavior at school or another institution. Ask them to share the situation and recount what they were thinking and feeling at the time. Then have them draw the situation they recounted, depicting what they were thinking and feeling without using words or symbols. The pictures can be as abstract or realistic as they wish. Ask questions about what they are drawing, what colors or shapes they will use for showing which feelings, and so on.

Ask them to take turns sharing their drawings, talking about what they drew and how they depicted their thoughts and feelings. Be sure to ask at least two questions to help each one explain his or her drawing and say at least two things about what you notice about the drawing. Ask questions such as the following:

- Was it more difficult to draw the feelings or the thoughts?
- What would you do differently now to avoid getting into trouble?
- What gets in the way of changing your behavior?
- To what extent would you blame someone else for your behavior (say that someone else's behavior made you do something that got you in trouble)?
- What have you learned in this group that might help you try a more appropriate behavior?

Sometimes recounting bad experiences can be hard for participants, either because of the feelings that are associated with them or because they minimize the feelings and do not view the experience as a problem. Encourage them to identify an experience even if they cannot remember the first such time.

Group members often draw actual representations of the situations. While this is certainly acceptable, encourage them to move on to abstract representations. This tends to help them tap more deeply into their thoughts and feelings. It can also help them to experience flexibility.

71.
Mind Talk

GOALS ▶
- Group members understand self-talk (mind talk).
- Group members can consciously use self-talk strategies.

DESCRIPTION ▶
Group members generate a list of positive self-talk messages.

MATERIALS NEEDED ▶
None.

DIRECTIONS ▶
Explain that mind talk—or self-talk—is the thoughts that people have about themselves and the messages that they give to themselves. These may be either negative or positive. Ask the group for examples. Write all the messages they think of on a chalkboard or newsprint, including those that are negative. Next, ask participants to identify the messages that help them overcome problematic situations. Ask them what would happen if they focused on these messages.

Draw arrows from each negative mind-talk message to any corresponding positive messages on the board or newsprint. Explain that we want to talk ourselves into doing the positive and healthy thing in any given circumstance. Ask the group to come up with more positive messages until they reach fifty positive mind-talk messages.

Lead a discussion, asking questions such as the following:

- What feelings does each message trigger in you?
- How can you transform negative messages into positive messages?
- What helps you decide to use mind talk when you are faced with a problematic situation?

THINGS TO THINK ABOUT ▶
Some young people find it very difficult to focus on self-talk before they act. They may say, "I just don't think about the stuff I do." Let them know that most of us have not trained ourselves to notice what we say to ourselves before we act, but that we do generally have thoughts, or self-talk, before we take actions. Give them some examples to illustrate. Encourage group members to feel comfortable identifying what goes through their heads and how this can help them make healthier decisions.

Negative Self-messages:

- This guy's not going to get one over on me.
- I have to prove I'm in control.
- I'm going to do something to this jerk to get him back.

Positive Self-messages:

- It's not worth it to get into a fight.
- I don't have to prove anything. I already know I'm okay.
- I have better things to do with my time than get him back.

MY OBSERVATIONS ▶

72.
The Only Person I Can Control Is Myself

Recommended
ages: 10 +

Phase 3

GOALS

- Group members increase their understanding of what they can and cannot control.
- Group members take more responsibility for their own actions.

DESCRIPTION

Participants try to make a partner fold a piece of paper two times.

MATERIALS NEEDED

A paper clip and a piece of paper for each group member.

DIRECTIONS

Begin a discussion with group members regarding things in their lives that they can control. First ask them to identify internal things they cannot control (blood flow, heartbeat). Contrast this with things they can partially control (blinking, holding their breath). Then move on to external things they cannot control (weather, other people's feelings). Examine the difference between influencing a situation and controlling it.

Place a paper clip in front of each participant. Have them bend it to make a shape of their choosing. Ask them about their ability to control how they shaped the paper clip.

Next, have group members pair up. Have each pair decide who goes first. Give each pair two pieces of paper. The person going first has one minute to "make" the other person fold one piece of paper two times. They can do anything but touch each other. Then have the pairs switch roles.

Ask the group to describe what happened in their pairs, using questions such as the following:

- Did anyone fold the paper?
- What influenced them to do so?
- What did they tell themselves?
- Did anyone "make" anyone else do anything?
- To what degree did anyone control anything in this situation?
- Did anyone else control you?
- If you say, "If so-and-so hadn't pushed me, I wouldn't have hit him," are you suggesting that person controls you?
- Can other people control your response to them?

**THINGS TO
THINK ABOUT** ▶

**MY
OBSERVATIONS** ▶

Emphasize that the only people they controlled in this activity were themselves. Discuss the fact that if anyone folded the paper, it was because they were influenced, not controlled. Draw the connection for the participants that blaming their behavior on someone else's actions is the same as saying the other person controls them.

It may be helpful with older group members to discuss the difference between "I can't" statements, which indicate a belief that one is not in control of oneself, and "I won't" statements, which indicate that one is taking responsibility for one's actions.

_____

_____

_____

_____

_____

_____

_____

_____

_____

_____

_____

73.
I Just Reacted

GOALS	■	Group members increase their ability to recognize the thoughts they have before reacting.
	■	Group members recognize that they are responsible for their actions.

DESCRIPTION

Group members identify the thoughts that lead to reactions that, at first, seem automatic.

MATERIALS NEEDED

None.

DIRECTIONS

Ask group members to talk about situations they have experienced where they believe they reacted "automatically." These reactions could be a violent act or other immediate response to an external stimulus. If they have trouble coming up with an experience, ask them to name situations in which they imagine they would react reflexively. List the situations they come up with on the chalkboard or newsprint.

Ask them to identify their thoughts just before they reacted (or what their thoughts might be if they came up with hypothetical situations). Most often they will say that they did not think, they "just reacted." Explain that everybody thinks—be it for nanoseconds or for long periods of time—before they take any action. Point out that people are not always aware of these thoughts because they sometimes occur so quickly. Note that the only exceptions are automatic body functions such as digesting food or the heart beating.

Have group members choose from the list the three situations they think are the best examples of "just reacting." Next, ask the group to choose the situation they think is most likely to generate the impulse to just react. Write across the top of the board "Thought," "Decisions," "Thought," "Reaction." Draw lines between each of the words. Now starting on the far right side of the board, under "Reaction," write the specific reaction behavior that the group identified. Then, moving to the far left under the first "Thought," write three thoughts that the group members guess might have gone through the head of the person who reacted. Under "Decisions," write the decisions that the group members say were made from the initial thoughts. Finally, ask group members what thoughts are sent to various body parts to actually carry out a behavior that is a reaction to the situation. Write these in the third column.

Ask the group to discuss the thinking process that precedes reacting, using questions such as the following:

- What requires thought before acting?
- How would you explain this process to a parent or a friend?
- If you believe that you always think before acting, does this mean you have choices in what you do?
- Who is in control of your choices and actions?
- Why do some people say they just reacted, or were out of control, when they realize that they hurt someone?
- What does responsibility have to do with this?

THINGS TO THINK ABOUT ▶

It is critical that participants understand that thoughts precede their actions, even when the thoughts are lightning fast. This is what will allow them to take responsibility for their actions.

If the group does not understand or does not buy that thoughts come before feelings, which in turn come before actions, ask them to collectively develop a situation in which it seems like a person reacted without thought. Then dissect the process. You might use an example of an elderly person home alone at night who awakens suddenly to a loud crash in the kitchen. Ask what the person might be feeling. (The group will probably answer fear, horror, or anger.) Ask what the person would be thinking that would lead him or her to those feelings? (Someone is breaking in.) Then pose the idea that, when the elderly person is awakened, the thought that comes to mind is "Oh, it's that darn cat again." Ask what feelings would result in that case.

As another example, some group members may argue that pushing back is an automatic reaction. You can then ask why they don't kick, bite, scratch, or, for that matter, run away instead when they are pushed. Usually they will say, "Oh, that's fighting like a sissy or a punk," or "You gotta show them they can't push you around." This demonstrates that a thought precedes the decision to push.

MY OBSERVATIONS ▶

_____

_____

_____

_____

_____

_____

74.
Tug-of-choice

GOALS ▶
- Group members understand that they have control over their behaviors and can make choices about them.
- Group members increase their understanding of how they make choices.
- Group members develop additional ways to make choices in response to what others do.

DESCRIPTION ▶

Using a length of rope, participants try to pull each other off narrow pieces of wood.

MATERIALS NEEDED ▶

Two pieces of two-by-four lumber, each about two-and-a-half or three feet long, and one piece of rope, about five feet long.

DIRECTIONS ▶

Place the two pieces of two-by-four lumber flat on the floor parallel to each other and about four to six feet apart. Have one group member balance on each piece of wood so that they are facing each other. Give each person one end of a five-foot rope. The participants use the rope to try to pull each other off the lumber. The person who stays on the piece of wood takes on a new challenger until everyone in the group has had a turn. The rules: You cannot talk. You can only use the rope to get the other person off the board. Once a person falls or touches the ground, the round is over. The facilitator is the final judge.

After everyone has had a turn standing on the piece of wood and trying to pull the other person off, have the group sit in a circle and ask questions such as the following:

- What choices did some of the group members make in order to get their opponent off the lumber?
- How many attempts did it take on average?
- What style was most successful?
- When someone tries to pull or push you, what is your natural reaction?
- Did everyone follow the rules?
- Did anyone feel like they wanted to stay on top no matter what?

Guide the discussion so participants will understand that they make choices regarding all their behaviors, no matter how much it feels like they are simply reacting to others. We are always in control of these behaviors, and only we are responsible for these behaviors.

Stay aware of how physical this process is. Remain as referee, providing structure and opportunity for members to try the activity. This increases the feeling of safety, and potentially the participation, among group members.

Many members step up to the spot and want to demonstrate how tough or strong they are. Focus on how this attitude affects the rest of the group. If the attitude is obstructing the activity, stop it temporarily and ask questions such as the following:

- Does anyone notice any tension within the group?
- What do you think is the source of this tension?
- I noticed that some of you see this as a highly competitive activity. How could this affect others' participation?
- How can we increase the feeling of safety for everyone so all group members will be willing to participate?

Do not wait to address behaviors that seem aggressive. If you let one or two things go by, it sends a message that a certain amount of aggressiveness is acceptable here.

**MY
OBSERVATIONS** ▶

_____

_____

_____

_____

_____

_____

_____

_____

_____

75.
Responsible Behavior Plans

Recommended
ages: 10 +

Phase 3

GOALS

- Group members understand the value of being responsible for their own behavior.
- Group members create a plan to take responsibility for their own behavior.
- Group members have a strategy for using nonviolent means to meet their needs.

DESCRIPTION

Group members develop a behavior plan for responding appropriately to problematic situations.

MATERIALS NEEDED

A copy of the Responsible Behavior Chart (page 184) for each group member, pencils, and Circle of Courage talking piece.

DIRECTIONS ▶

Have group members share, in a Circle of Courage (see page 35), a time when they were told that they had been hurtful to someone else. They may or may not agree that their behavior had been hurtful. Still, it was seen by someone as having been hurtful. Make sure the sharing stays objective and nonblaming. Record the basic situation related by each group member on the chalkboard or newsprint. Go around the circle again looking at each situation recorded on the board and ask the members in turn to say how they would feel and what they would think if this behavior were done to them.

Pass out the Responsible Behavior Chart and pencils to the participants. Explain that this chart helps them prepare for making positive and healthy choices. Have participants write a difficult situation they have faced in the situation column. Then have them write (1) the thoughts they had in this situation; (2) the feelings they had; (3) the intensity of this situation on a scale of one to ten, one being the least intense and ten being the most; (4) the choices they had when they encountered this situation.

You may have to talk this through with each group member within the large group. This would allow you to get input from other group members. When everyone has completed their charts, ask them to go around the circle and share the charts. Lead a discussion asking questions such as the following:

- What was the most difficult part of this activity?
- How might this information help you in future situations?
- What additions can you make to your choices now?
- Who have you seen use this process in real life?
- What supports might you have in this process?

Developing these plans is a critical part of the curriculum. Having participants refer to these plans during the rest of the time you spend with them can reinforce the options that participants are willing to try and feel they can do. Remember that if they feel they can carry out an option, they are more likely to try it. If they feel powerless over their situation and the others in the situation, they are less likely to try something new.

Some group members will probably resist putting anything on paper. If they do put something on paper, it often will be sketchy at best. Avoid being judgmental about what they write. If they can use the form to verbalize the process, they have accomplished a great deal.

MY OBSERVATIONS ▶

_____

_____

_____

_____

_____

_____

_____

_____

_____

_____

_____

_____

_____

Responsible Behavior Chart

Situation	Thoughts	Feelings	Intensity	Choices

76.
Healthy Choices

Recommended ages: 10 +

Phase 3

GOALS

- Group members better understand the idea of making choices.
- Group members develop increased understanding of how to make healthy choices.

DESCRIPTION

Group members list choices people have to make and identify which are healthy and which are unhealthy.

MATERIALS NEEDED

None.

DIRECTIONS

Draw two columns on the chalkboard or newsprint. Ask participants to name significant people in their lives, such as parents, teachers, or other adults. List these in the left-hand column. Ask participants to name the types of choices these adults have to make and list the choices in the right-hand column. The choices might involve things such as getting up from bed, going to work, eating lunch, reading the paper, deciding what to make for supper, scheduling transportation for their children's activities, smoking, drinking, using drugs, and so on. Finally, ask the group to indicate to you which of these choices are healthy choices and which are not.

Next, ask the group to name choices they need to make in their lives right now. These could include things such as when to get up, what cereal to eat for breakfast, whether to listen to directions in school, how to treat certain peers, what activities to get involved in, and so on. Write these on the board or newsprint as they are named.

Have the group members identify which are healthy choices and circle them. Discuss what goes into making a healthy choice, asking questions such as the following:

- How do you decide you will make a healthy choice?
- What kinds of rewards might you get if you make a healthy choice?
- Who influences you when making a healthy choice?
- Do you think about what someone else might do before you choose to do something?
- Do you ever consult with anyone else?

Next, have them list some of the obstacles to making healthy choices.

Try to have participants identify choices that they are most familiar with. You may need to emphasize that many of the choices they make seem minor, such as choosing whether or not to put bananas on their cereal or which side of the street to walk on. It may be difficult for them to make the connection between these specific choices and the whole idea of making healthy choices. In fact, thinking about healthy choices may be a new experience for group members. Be patient with the process. This is another activity in which you are simply planting seeds that will surface in the future.

Help group members understand that often the obstacles to making healthy choices are rooted in people's thoughts, in what they tell themselves.

**MY
OBSERVATIONS** ▶

_____

_____

_____

_____

_____

_____

_____

_____

_____

_____

_____

_____

_____

77.
Choice Web

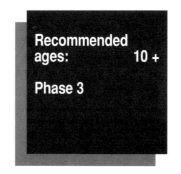
Recommended ages: 10 +

Phase 3

GOALS ▶	■ Group members better understand how one choice follows from another. ■ Group members are better able to think through their choices.
DESCRIPTION ▶	Group members draw a map of how any one choice they make affects the other choices they have.
MATERIALS NEEDED ▶	Two sheets of paper for each group member, pencils, and crayons, colored pencils, or markers.
DIRECTIONS ▶	Explain that every choice a person makes leads to at least one other possible choice, which in turn affects another set of choices. Tell participants they will be drawing a map based on the following situation: You got up this morning and decided that you were going to have cereal for breakfast. As you were preparing your breakfast, you noticed that you were running late. As you finished eating your cereal, you saw the bus leave. You chased after it, but it went on to school without you.

Give each participant a sheet of paper and drawing materials. Give directions as follows.

1. Draw a circle centered at the top of the page and write "eat breakfast" inside the circle.
2. Draw a short line from the first circle to a second circle.
3. Write "missed bus" along the line.
4. Write "kicked nearby tree" inside the second circle.
5. From the second circle, draw two more lines with circles at the end of each.
6. Write "hurt foot" on one of the lines.
7. In the circle at the end of that line, write "continue to limp home."
8. On the second line write "What am I going to do?"
9. In the circle at the end of the second line, write "start walking to school."
10. Continue to draw lines and circles illustrating actions and new choices until there are at least four levels of choices stemming from the first choice of eating breakfast.

Pass out another piece of paper. This time describe the following situation:

You get to school, and the first person you see is someone you have made fun of before. As you walk by this person, you . . .

1. Draw a circle centered at the top of your paper and write in it the choice you will make in response to this situation.
2. Repeat the steps that you took in the first exercise until you again have four levels of choices and actions.

When participants have completed their maps, ask each group member to describe the thoughts and feelings that led up to the next choice. Ask questions such as the following:

- Were there some choices you made that led to negative consequences?
- What were they?
- Were there some choices you made that led to positive outcomes?
- What were they?
- What choices would you make toward positive outcomes if you were to continue?
- What do you notice about choice making when you see these situations in the web?

THINGS TO THINK ABOUT ▶

This activity can be eye opening for participants. Although they probably will not retain the information for very long initially, they will be able to draw on what they learned in the future.

You can use the choice web again if group members describe problematic situations. It can become an excellent tool for them when they are familiar with it.

MY OBSERVATIONS ▶

_____

_____

_____

_____

_____

_____

_____

78.
Knowing My Power

GOALS ▶
- Group members begin to understand the different kinds of power that exist.
- Group members become familiar with their own power and how to use it positively.

DESCRIPTION ▶
Group members attempt to assemble a flashlight without knowing what they are assembling.

MATERIALS NEEDED ▶
A flashlight that has been disassembled into as many parts as possible.

DIRECTIONS ▶
Ask group members to share their definitions of power and write these on the chalkboard or newsprint. Ask them to describe the various ways power is used and who most often uses it, who tends not to have power, how power can be used in positive ways, and how it can be used in negative ways.

Pass out a piece of the flashlight to each person in the group. Tell them they have two minutes to assemble this item (do not use the word *flashlight*). They can only assemble it one piece at a time, and they cannot pool the pieces. At the end of two minutes, ask them questions such as the following:

- What types of power were exhibited in assembling the flashlight?
- Who seemed to have the most power during the assembly process?
- Who seemed to have the least power?
- Where did the overall power lie in this process?
- Where is the power in the flashlight itself?
- What needs to happen to access the power?

THINGS TO THINK ABOUT ▶
Group members may say power is always negative or say they never have power themselves. Emphasize the fact that some people have more power than others, for example, adults over children or a boss over employees. Sometimes this is a necessary structure. Sometimes we allow others to have more power because of their experience and wisdom. It is when the power is misused that it is abusive.

There are two types of power being referred to in this activity. The first is the power of group members themselves; the second is the power within the flashlight. Although the batteries contain the energy to light the bulb, all components are equally necessary for the flashlight to work.

MY OBSERVATIONS ▶

79.
Peaceful Alphabet

GOAL

- Group members develop peaceful alternatives to using bullying behaviors.

DESCRIPTION

Each group member creates a book of twenty-six different behaviors that represent peaceful alternatives to bullying behaviors.

MATERIALS NEEDED

At least twenty-six pieces of blank paper for each participant, pencils, and colored pencils, markers, or crayons.

DIRECTIONS

Write the letters of the alphabet vertically on the chalkboard or newsprint. Ask group members to brainstorm ways to act peacefully in situations when they might otherwise use violent or bullying behaviors. They must think of an alternative for every letter of the alphabet. Write all of their ideas on the chalkboard or newsprint. Then pass out twenty-six pieces of paper to each participant. Have them write a different word, phrase, or sentence on each page, each one representing a different letter of the alphabet, and then draw a picture or design to represent the idea.

This activity may take a portion of several sessions. During the drawing and designing of pages, you can engage participants in discussions regarding how they are choosing to show these options on their pages.

When they have completed their peaceful alphabet books, ask them to choose the five letters and pictures that they like to use most and share these with the group.

THINGS TO THINK ABOUT

Your guidance in making the list is very important. Some possibilities for the use of letters are: A is for *Assertively address the person.* B is for *Believe and think about a way out of the situation that is not hurtful to me or the other person.* C is for *Calm myself when it feels like my buttons are getting pushed.* D is for *Deliver a positive and appropriate message about how I feel.* E is for *Express myself in a clear and positive manner,* and so on.

Some participants may hesitate because this activity involves drawing. Reassure them that they can use simple shapes, colors, or symbolic representations. The ability to draw realistically is not important.

MY OBSERVATIONS

80.
Tough Times

GOALS ▶

- Group members become aware of the cognitive skills they use to address difficult situations.
- Group members increase their options for addressing difficult situations.

DESCRIPTION ▶

Group members identify situations that have been tough for them and develop and practice solutions.

MATERIALS NEEDED ▶

Paper, drawing materials, and Circle of Courage talking piece.

DIRECTIONS ▶

Ask participants to sit in a Circle of Courage (see page 35). Ask them to take turns responding to the statement: "One of the toughest situations I have ever been in was . . ." When everyone has taken a turn, ask the group to respond to a second statement: "The thing that really made this a tough situation was . . ." Finally, ask them to respond to a third statement: "One of the things I thought about that helped me get through the situation in a safe way was . . ."

Write on the chalkboard or newsprint the thoughts that helped them get through the situation in a safe way. Ask questions such as the following:

- What similarities do you notice in the things group members shared?
- Did you ever have any of the thoughts that other group members talked about having?
- Besides your being safe, how did the situation end up?
- If you were in a similar situation in the future, what other things might you say to yourself to stay safe?
- What might you do differently?

Ask each group member to draw a picture of a situation that could happen in the future. Have them draw a speech balloon in the picture and fill in what they will say to themselves if this situation occurs.

Have participants take turns describing their pictures. Ask them questions such as the following:

- Can you name two choices you might have about how to behave in the situation you drew?
- What similarities are there between what people might think in these situations?
- What would be difficult about thinking it?
- What would keep you from thinking it?

THINGS TO THINK ABOUT ▶

You may need to help participants develop their ideas about tough situations they have experienced. Remind them to limit their initial sharing to the actual description of what happened. Group members may also have some difficulty identifying their thoughts during the situation. Provide them with some possible thoughts, such as the following:

- I don't need to get in trouble here.
- I'm feeling trapped. Who can I talk to about what is happening here?
- This is a hard situation, but I know I can get through it.

When participants begin drawing, let them know that their pictures can be as simple or complex as they want to make them.

MY OBSERVATIONS ▶

_____

_____

_____

_____

_____

_____

_____

_____

_____

_____

81.
Choosing to Respond or Share a Fact

Recommended ages: 10 +

Phase 3

GOAL ▶
- Group members increase their positive options for responding to difficult situations.

DESCRIPTION ▶
Group members take turns either stating a fact about themselves or acting out appropriately assertive responses to situations they draw out of a jar.

MATERIALS NEEDED ▶
A large piece of tagboard with instructions outlining assertive communication (see Guidelines for Assertive Communication on page 139); a slip of paper for each group member with a situation that could realistically happen in a school or other setting with peers or authority figures; and a jar to hold the slips of paper.

DIRECTIONS ▶
Have group members sit in a circle. Review the instructions for assertive communication with the group members. When you are finished post these guidelines in the room.

Tell participants they will go around the circle taking turns. They may choose to (1) select a slip of paper from the jar and explain or demonstrate an assertive response to the situation described on the paper, or (2) tell a fact about themselves.

If they choose to demonstrate an assertive response, they will pick a slip of paper out of the jar when it is their turn, read aloud the situation written on the paper, and describe or act out an assertive response. If they cannot think of an assertive response, they should ask the group to assist them. When the participant hears a response that is usable, he or she then acts it out or describes how to use the idea.

When everyone has had a turn, have the group members discuss how they experienced this activity using questions such as the following:

- How many times did people choose to say a fact about themselves? How many times did they choose to respond to a situation in an assertive manner? What did you notice about this?
- Was there anything difficult in sharing a fact about yourself?
- What was the most difficult part of responding?

**THINGS TO
THINK ABOUT** ▶

**MY
OBSERVATIONS** ▶

Be sure to provide encouragement and positive comments for all assertive responses. Point out even the subtle assertive behaviors and focus minimally on any reactions that might be negative or hurtful.

This is a good activity to use several times, but if you do this, you may want to keep adding slips of paper with new situations.

_____

_____

_____

_____

_____

_____

_____

_____

_____

_____

_____

_____

_____

_____

_____

82.
Writing Group Stories

Recommended ages: 10 +

Phase 3

GOALS ▶	■ Group members respond to situations in appropriate and nonviolent ways. ■ Group members appreciate the benefits of cooperation. ■ Group members understand why making connections with others is important.
DESCRIPTION ▶	Group members take turns contributing sentences to produce stories about young people facing difficult situations.
MATERIALS NEEDED ▶	Three sheets of newsprint, pens or markers, and a tape recorder (optional).
DIRECTIONS ▶	On the top of each sheet of newsprint, start three separate stories with one or two sentences. Following are some examples:

- Two days ago, Jennifer was called into the principal's office because of something that happened between her and Jeff. As she sat there, she had a lot of feelings.
- Pat loved to play on the playground. One day, Pat was lying on the ground looking up at the sky when, all of a sudden, two older kids stood over him.
- Jaime was with three friends when one of them suggested that they find some other kids to make fun of. Jaime thought that the kids probably wouldn't like this, so she decided she'd come up with some other suggestions.

Ask for volunteers to read the sentences at the top of one paper. Ask the students to go around the circle and each add one sentence to the story. Sometimes participants' contributions will not be realistic. Allow them to provide whatever sentence they wish, even if it is implausible or even harmful to the character in the story. Ask each group member to write his or her sentences on the newsprint. Alternately, you may read the initial sentences into a tape recorder, then have group members record each sentence they add. When everyone has shared a sentence or thought, you can bring the story to an end with one or two final thoughts or sentences. Read the entire story to the group or, if you recorded it, let the group listen to the story.

Put some parameters on the next story. Explain that you want them to contribute thoughts that help the main character to peacefully and appropriately address his or her concerns. Ask the group to focus on positive and safe options. Repeat the process as carried out with the first story.

Discuss the situation after the group has listened to the entire story. Ask questions such as the following:

- What types of options were offered for the main character?
- What types of feelings might this person have had?
- Has anybody here ever experienced a situation like this before?
- What are some other things that could have been included in the story?
- How would these additions have changed the outcome?
- Did you hear suggestions from other group members for dealing with the dilemma in the story that you hadn't thought of?
- Do you think you can benefit from hearing other people's ideas?

Try this activity a third time and follow the same procedure. The group members' ability to develop stronger options will increase as they gain experience with this activity.

THINGS TO THINK ABOUT ▶

Use the tape recorder option if group members have trouble with reading or writing.

At times, group members may try to make this story gross or tremendously unrealistic. Allow them to go anywhere they want with the first story and offer your observations regarding the probable effects of the suggested behaviors.

MY OBSERVATIONS ▶

_____

_____

_____

_____

_____

_____

_____

_____

_____

83.
What Would I Tell a Friend in Trouble?

Recommended ages: 10 +

Phase 3

GOAL	▶	■ Group members increase their positive options for responding to difficult situations.
DESCRIPTION	▶	Group members brainstorm a list of fifty positive options for a friend who is being pushed around. When finished, they prioritize the list and role-play the options.
MATERIALS NEEDED	▶	None.
DIRECTIONS	▶	Describe a scenario for the group members in which a friend is being pushed around at school. Tell the group they have three minutes to create a list of fifty positive options they could suggest to their friend for handling the difficult situation. When you say "go," everyone will shout out options. Quickly write their options on a chalkboard or newsprint.

Next, explain that participants have only a minute to help the friend before they go to their next class, so they can choose only five of the options. Allow them a few minutes to choose the five options as a group. You may need to assist them in maintaining a focus on positive and appropriate alternatives. Underline the options they select.

Tell group members that the friend came back later to report that only one of the suggestions had any effect on the person doing the pushing. Ask them to decide on three more possibilities to suggest. Underline the next three options they select.

Process this activity, asking questions such as the following:

■ Is it easier to provide a friend with positive suggestions than to choose a positive alternative for yourself?
■ If the friend decides to respond to the pushing with violence, what would you tell the friend to consider?
■ What sort of trouble could the friend get into?
■ Can the friend ever be guaranteed that the other person will stop pushing?
■ If not, what can the friend control?

Next, ask for two volunteers to role-play a situation in which one of them is advising the other, who has been getting pushed around. Ask the adviser to choose an option from the list and suggest it to the other person. Then, ask the other person to insist that he or she has already tried the suggestion or that it "wouldn't work." Have the adviser continue to choose options from the list, repeating the process. Remind the group that the goal of providing options is not necessarily to stop the hurtful behavior, but to give the friend some practical tools that can help keep him or her safe and out of trouble.

Ask the group what they saw in this role play. Ask them what was most helpful about what the adviser did for the friend.

THINGS TO THINK ABOUT 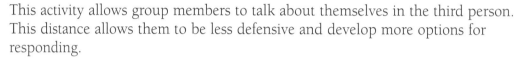 This activity allows group members to talk about themselves in the third person. This distance allows them to be less defensive and develop more options for responding.

Group members may have few ideas initially. The time limits put an artificial pressure on the group to produce information and encourage them to work quickly. You can also set up an imaginary competition with previous groups by letting them know that the record number of options discovered in three minutes is forty-five. However, you may need to extend a time limit if you observe important information being shared.

Group members may argue with you about what options are realistic. Avoid discussing whether they are realistic; instead, remind participants that all positive, nonviolent options are at least worth considering.

Some of the options contributed by the group members may be inappropriate and even violent. Guide their contributions by accepting the ideas and reframing them in a way that is positive. For example, should one of the group members suggest that the friend should get some other big guys and go beat up the person who was bullying, you can suggest that it is a good idea to connect with other friends and then figure out what might be supportive to this friend, rather than what might hurt someone else.

MY OBSERVATIONS

_____

_____

_____

_____

_____

84.
Pushing Hands

Recommended
ages: 10 +

Phase 3

GOALS ▶

- Group members understand the natural reaction to being pushed.
- Group members increase their positive options for responding to difficult situations.

DESCRIPTION ▶

Group members push against each other's hands and make observations about the experience.

MATERIALS NEEDED ▶

None.

DIRECTIONS ▶

First, ask group members if they are able to identify more than one way to respond in situations where they feel they are getting attacked.

Have group members pair up and stand facing each other. Ask one member of each pair to take the role of the pusher. Have the pairs raise their hands so their palms are facing each other but not touching. Explain that when you say "go," the pusher is to push against the other's hands as hard as he or she can. When you say "stop," both participants are to freeze in their positions, look around the room, and note what other people are doing. When you are sure everyone understands the directions, say, "Ready, set, go." Allow only a few seconds, then say "stop." Ask them to look around at how people are standing in relation to each other, at their posture, at the positions of their feet, or at any other significant aspect of their appearance. Let the group members unfreeze and sit down.

Discuss the experience asking questions such as the following:

- What did you see about people's body positions?
- Did you notice any ways that people were preparing themselves even before I said "go"?
- What were the rules for the people who were to push?
- What did you hear me tell the receivers of the pushing to do? (The answer is "nothing"; you gave no directions to the receivers of the pushing. This makes the point that pushing back is a natural response. Try to emphasize that most of us have a tendency to react in this way.)

Next, choose a group member to assist you in a demonstration. The group member will be the pusher; you will receive the pushing. Give the participant the same directions about pushing that you gave previously. When you say "go," immediately throw your hands down so no contact is made. The pusher will often fall into you. Start again and say "go." This time grab the pusher's hands and begin dancing together. Make it lighthearted and fun, perhaps even add some singing. Have the other person prepare one more time. Encourage this person to get ready to push really hard on your hands. When you say "go," turn around and run away a few steps. Thank the person for helping you in the demonstration and have him or her sit down.

Ask the group members questions such as the following:

- What did you observe in this demonstration?
- What were the options I chose rather than pushing back? (Remind them that the directions were still given only to the pusher.)
- What made it easier for me to choose three other options? (Practice; I knew what was coming; I was thinking about how I was going to respond.)
- Are there other options I could have used? (Explain that you could have chosen to push back, but you chose other behaviors. You had to think through your choices. If you had reacted without thinking, you might have pushed back; that, too, would have been a choice.)
- What gets in the way of thinking about other options when you feel someone is pushing you?
- What makes using nonviolent choices unrealistic? (Is it because they never work? Do violent choices work?)
- Which options might get you in trouble?
- Which options might get you out of the situation without getting you into trouble?

Point out to group members that if they went fishing and didn't catch anything with the bait they were using, they probably would try another type of bait the next time. People can choose other courses of action even though they might feel more comfortable with the same old ways.

THINGS TO THINK ABOUT

This activity can be powerful in teaching that participants may choose to use the most readily available response, even if it is problematic, but they don't have to. The follow-up discussion can help them become aware of thinking processes that they have not been able to identify.

It is important to describe the rules clearly and emphatically for this activity while participants are standing, and then move quickly to the exercise. You want participants to respond as spontaneously as possible. If you allow too much time between the instructions and the activity, some group members may lose motivation and excitement. Some participants may also figure out how to push the other person too hard.

A pusher may try to hurt another person. Usually, the receiver finds ways to avoid this. However, should this happen, use the situation to talk about how the receiver was feeling or what he or she was thinking. This type of processing allows everyone an opportunity to learn. Calling attention to this type of behavior in a nonshaming manner can also give feedback to the person who did the pushing. While there is a chance that someone could be hurt in this activity, you can reduce the risk by quickly saying "stop." Another option is to use only one or two pairs as examples to the rest of the group. Your knowledge of the group members should allow you to reduce the possibility of someone getting hurt.

Some will say that when you are in a fight, there are no options but to fight back. Otherwise you look like a wimp (or other derogatory term for a weak person). Respond by asking if a person always looks weak if they try some other option. If the group members identify an alternative that does not look weak, ask for more examples of how people can get out of fighting without hurting or getting hurt. If all the group members insist there are no other options, remind them of the three alternatives you demonstrated. Ask them what makes those examples unrealistic or unusable.

Avoid pressuring them into giving you the answer you want to hear. If they do not agree with you, acknowledge that you understand they do not see any options other than fighting. Let them know that fighting puts them at a higher risk of getting into trouble, hurting someone else, or getting hurt themselves. State clearly that you can see other options that can be used to reduce the risks, but in the end it is up to them which behaviors they will use. If necessary, end the activity by agreeing to disagree.

MY OBSERVATIONS ▶

85.
Survival Life

GOALS

- Group members are able to identify when they are actually faced with a life-or-death situation.
- Group members increase their repertoire of assertive behaviors.

DESCRIPTION

Group members distinguish between life-or-death situations and those that only feel like it. They brainstorm nonviolent options for maintaining safety.

MATERIALS NEEDED

None.

DIRECTIONS

Lead a discussion about situations in which people are faced with survival decisions, asking questions such as the following:

- Can you think of a situation in which violence is the only response that can ensure a person's survival?
- What people are usually in these types of situations?
- What television shows depict people in these survival situations?
- What does the main character often do to take care of him- or herself? (Note that the main character frequently is given permission to be violent because of the need to survive or to save someone else's life.)

Ask participants the following questions: "Have you experienced times when it felt like your personal safety would be at stake if you did not defend yourself with violence?" "Do you know people who felt they had to defend their survival with violence?" Allow the situations to be briefly described and list key phrases on the chalkboard or newsprint. Some of these key phrases will be: "I had to," "I just reacted," or "If I didn't do what I needed to, someone would be hurt or dead."

Chances are good that the participants will give examples that were not actually survival situations, even though they felt like it to them. By doing so, they may be creating a rationale for a violent response that they believe was appropriate and that they then generalize to less threatening times as well. Help them to determine whether the situation was actually a life-and-death one. Note that very rarely are our lives threatened, and even on the rare occasions when they are, people frequently have more options than responding with violence.

Read the following situation aloud:

Sam is walking home from school. Usually, he avoids going down Elm Street because there's an older kid who lives there who runs out when he sees Sam and starts pushing him around. He has threatened Sam with a knife, which Sam has never seen. Today, Sam wants to get home fast because his grandmother is taking him to a special event, so he takes the risk and goes down Elm Street. Sure enough, the older boy sees Sam, runs up behind him, and grabs him. Sam stops and turns around. The older boy tells Sam to give him some money. Sam refuses. The boy puts his hand in his pocket and says he'll use his knife on Sam if he doesn't give him money. Sam still refuses. The other boy begins taking his hand out of his pocket and Sam sees what appears to be a metal object. Sam sees a broken tree limb near him on the ground. He also notices that a few people have stepped out of their houses. Sam knows he can't run faster than the boy.

Ask each group member, one at a time, what thoughts Sam might be having, what feelings Sam might be having, and what options Sam might have. After these options have been shared, ask the group members to describe how they would feel about using one of these options in this situation. If the options do not seem realistic to them, or if they would not choose the options identified, help them talk about what barriers there are to finding alternatives. Resistance to accepting alternatives often has to do with feeling hopeless and helpless. Consider raising this point with group members.

THINGS TO THINK ABOUT ▶

Probably, few group members will have really examined the situations that seemed life threatening to them. Since many of the situations are not actually life threatening, helping participants to identify the stakes in the situation (frequently saving face) and the possibility of nonviolent responses can be eye opening for them.

Make sure you emphasize how rare survival situations are in real life, even in the most seemingly dangerous schools in the country.

Some people believe this exercise will heighten young people's fears and exacerbate violence. It may promote an increase in discussion; however, it is rare that talking about a situation in a structured manner will ever bring about an increase in violence. Structure and guidance are key.

MY OBSERVATIONS ▶

_____

_____

_____

_____

_____

86.
Walking Away
When You Can

Recommended
ages: 10 +

Phase 3

GOALS

- Group members understand what feeling triggers are.
- Group members are prepared to respond appropriately to triggers.
- Group members walk away more frequently in problematic situations.
- Group members increase their options for responding to difficult situations.

DESCRIPTION

Group members draw feeling triggers and positive responses from jars and role-play their selections.

MATERIALS NEEDED

A jar with enough slips of paper containing trigger words or situations for half the group. Examples include name-calling ("punk," "jerk"), swearing, put-downs ("You're dumb"; "Girls are always spacey"), threats ("You'd better give me your money or I'll . . ."), and intimidating remarks ("Who do you think you are?"; "Watch it, Dude").

You'll also need a jar with at least three slips of paper for each member in the other half of the group that contain appropriate responses to triggers. Examples include walking away, using self-talk ("This is not worth it"; "I have better things to do"; "I don't need to get more detention"; "I need to get an adult involved to help"; "This doesn't feel safe to me right now"; "I need some space"; "I feel . . ."; "I can stay in control"; "I can call . . . "; "Even though I feel alone and accused, I can hold it together until I get out of here"), and going immediately to a school staff person or another adult to talk through feelings and how the situation was experienced.

DIRECTIONS

Point out to the group that one helpful way to respond to a difficult situation is to walk away. Ask the group what makes a situation tough to walk away from. Look for answers such as these: "You can't let others get away with things"; "You gotta let others know where you stand"; "I just get so upset I blow up"; "When people start pushing my buttons—by what they say, by trying to put me down, or by not listening—I just get mad"; "The other person is getting in my face."

Discuss triggers. Tell group members that triggers are things that they tend to react to with a certain emotion, such as fear or anger. Another way of talking about triggers is by describing them as buttons that people seem to push. Actions, words, sights, smells, and so on can all become triggers when a person has had a negative experience with them. They can become signals that bring up the negative experience. Just because they are there doesn't mean people have to react the same way all the time. In fact, the same action or word may be seen as a trigger in some situations and not in others. Calling another guy "Dude" may have a different impact depending on the person it is being directed at. It is important to recognize your triggers and choose ahead of time how you will behave when you are confronted with them in the future.

Ask participants to name as many triggers as they can, then list them on the chalkboard or newsprint. Place a jar on a chair at either end of the room. One jar contains slips of paper that have possible triggers (words or actions). The other jar contains slips of paper that have positive options for responding to the trigger situations. Have half the group line up behind one jar and the other half behind the other jar. Ask the person at the front of the line behind the trigger jar to take a slip of paper, read it silently, and then say the trigger or act it out. The person at the front of the other line then takes a slip of paper out of the response jar and says or acts out the response. The participant may choose to pick two or three responses, if necessary, to get an option that fits for the situation. Allow every group member to take a turn.

Discuss the activity asking questions such as the following:

- What were the most difficult options?
- What other options could be included in the future?
- Which responses seemed more realistic?
- What adults in your life have modeled positive ways of responding to triggers?
- What might you think about next time you become aware of a trigger?

THINGS TO THINK ABOUT ▶

Having the group members identify their triggers can be extremely helpful to them. When their awareness is raised, they seem better able to develop coping tools.

Group members often want to focus on the most awful and difficult situations, including those that are life threatening. Explain that these types of situations rarely occur. State that the group will focus on the kinds of situations that occur most often, the ones where participants most frequently get themselves in trouble. However, you could let the group share a few very difficult situations to demonstrate that, even in especially challenging situations, a positive response is possible, and the positive response reduces the risk of getting in trouble, hurting someone else, or getting themselves hurt.

MY OBSERVATIONS ▶

_____

_____

_____

_____

_____

87.
Barriers to Successful Behavior

GOALS	■ Group members increase their understanding of their decision-making process.
	■ Group members increase their understanding of barriers to making good decisions.
	■ Group members better understand that stress can be a barrier.
	■ Group members begin to identify tools for making good choices.

DESCRIPTION

Group members dissect their decision-making process in a situation that did not turn out well, then discuss barriers they encountered.

MATERIALS NEEDED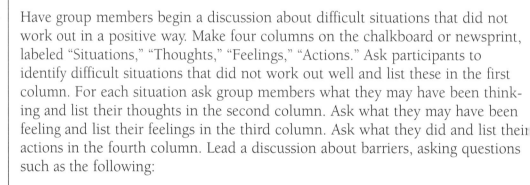

None.

DIRECTIONS

Have group members begin a discussion about difficult situations that did not work out in a positive way. Make four columns on the chalkboard or newsprint, labeled "Situations," "Thoughts," "Feelings," "Actions." Ask participants to identify difficult situations that did not work out well and list these in the first column. For each situation ask group members what they may have been thinking and list their thoughts in the second column. Ask what they may have been feeling and list their feelings in the third column. Ask what they did and list their actions in the fourth column. Lead a discussion about barriers, asking questions such as the following:

■ What were some of the barriers that were encountered?
■ What choices were being made when someone ran up against a barrier?
■ What was a difficult part of staying positive when you encountered a barrier or a wall?
■ When we feel pressured and stressed, what kinds of decisions are we apt to make?
■ In what ways are stress and pressure barriers in themselves?
■ How can someone choose to accept the barriers and make healthier choices?

**THINGS TO
THINK ABOUT** ▶

**MY
OBSERVATIONS** ▶

Help the group establish a basis for deciding what constitutes a barrier. Barriers could be stress, pressure, feelings of fear, confusion, frustration, and so on. However, emphasize that it may not really be the stress, pressure, or feelings that are the barriers, but the thinking that leads to them. One way participants can decrease the size of a barrier may be to change what they are thinking. Explain that they can use positive behaviors despite barriers.

88.
Stories of Peaceful Ways to Deal with Conflict

Recommended ages: 10 +

Phase 3

GOALS	■ Group members understand alternatives to violent behavior. ■ Group members develop personal options to violence.
DESCRIPTION	Group members identify techniques to resolve conflict peacefully through telling and diagramming stories.
MATERIALS NEEDED	None.
DIRECTIONS 	Ask the group members to spend one minute brainstorming their favorite television shows or movies. Write them on the chalkboard or newsprint as they call them out. Then ask them to pick a character in one of the movies or television shows to focus on. Ask them to identify what strategies this person used to peacefully address a situation in which there was conflict. They will probably not be able to come up with many; nevertheless, acknowledge any suggestions that apply even indirectly.

Then ask participants to share stories about someone in their lives who used a strategy to resolve a conflict with peaceful means. Have four participants take turns identifying the steps taken to make the decision to solve the problem peacefully in the stories they shared. Draw a horizontal line on the chalkboard or on a long piece of paper and label "start" and "end" at the appropriate places. As participants speak, diagram the process by drawing the actions and self-talk along the line, leading from the beginning of the conflict to the solution. Ask questions such as the following to help them dissect the process:

■ What similarities did you notice among the people participants identified?
■ Did these people all use the same strategies?
■ What actions did these people take?
■ What might they have told themselves in order to make the decision to solve the problem in a peaceful manner?

When the four stories are diagrammed, ask questions such as the following:

- What do you notice about the strategies people use?
- What do you notice about people's thoughts?
- What types of things seem easier to do in order to act in a peaceful manner?
- What are the things that get in the way of acting in a peaceful manner?
- Are there other things you can tell yourself in problematic situations that are helpful to you?

It is important to use the follow-up questions in this activity. It helps the participants deepen their understanding of others.

THINGS TO THINK ABOUT ▶

MY OBSERVATIONS ▶

_____

_____

_____

_____

_____

_____

_____

_____

_____

_____

_____

_____

_____

89.
How Do I Want to Be Treated When I Do Something Wrong?

Recommended ages: 10 +

Phase 3

GOALS ▶
- Group members envision ways to handle having made a mistake.
- Group members increase their options for addressing feelings following making mistakes.

DESCRIPTION ▶
Group members create a story together about a young person who does something wrong and is challenged by a teacher.

MATERIALS NEEDED ▶
None.

DIRECTIONS ▶
Have group members sit in a circle and begin a discussion about how they have experienced others' reactions to them when they do something wrong. For example, discuss the ways people talk to them or yell at them when they do something inappropriate or make a mistake. As they describe some of their experiences and observations, write them on a chalkboard or newsprint. Next, ask the group members for examples of respectful ways that people could treat them after they have done something that was hurtful to themselves or someone else.

Begin a story about a young person (the age of the group members present) who was caught playing a prank or joke on a smaller, younger child. A teacher or other adult caught this person and began to say . . . (here, ask participants to go around the circle adding to the story). When the story has gone around the circle at least once, ask questions such as the following:

- What did you hear happening in the story?
- What was the young person feeling like when he or she was being talked to by the adult?
- What does the story suggest about how this person felt he or she was treated (respected or not)?
- What else could the adult have said or done in this case?
- How can a teacher or other authority figure set limits for a young person and, at the same time, provide support and nurturing?
- What other supports might be helpful for this young person?
- What might this person have been thinking during this whole process?

THINGS TO THINK ABOUT

You can also use the Circle of Courage (see page 35) for this activity. Have the group members respond to the above questions.

It is sometimes helpful for group members to picture the young person in the story as their friend. This makes the story more personal without making anyone feel too vulnerable.

MY OBSERVATIONS

90.
Possible Endings to Impossible Situations

Recommended
ages: 10 +

Phase 3

GOAL ▶

- Group members increase their positive options for responding to difficult situations.

DESCRIPTION ▶

Group members match appropriate responses to difficult situations.

MATERIALS NEEDED ▶

Impossible-to-get-out-of Situations/Response Options list (see page 213). Make copies for each group member.

DIRECTIONS ▶

Ask the group to match the assertive response choices with the situations as quickly as possible. The group may either make the decisions after some discussion, or they may choose to vote on the matches. You should assist them in discussing the situations and the responses, but do not provide input on which response goes with which situation. As is evident, there are many correct answers. Nearly any response could go with any situation, and some of the situations may require two or three responses. No one way of responding will fix the situation in the long term. The basic point is that reacting in a negative or hurtful way will continue the cycle of hurt and pain, while choosing to do something different can help young people get out of this cycle.

After the group has made its decisions, ask questions such as the following:

- What was the most difficult part of this activity?
- Did being timed affect how the group worked on this activity?
- Were some responses more realistic in some situations than in others?
- Did it matter which person you were responding to?
- Did you feel your signals going off?
- How can you take care of yourself even when you have intense and angry feelings?
- What are some other responses you could add to the list?

THINGS TO THINK ABOUT ▶

Adapt this list to your own group's needs. Take time to add as many other appropriate responses as possible. Numbering the responses and lettering the situations could be an easy and quick way for group members to match them up.

MY OBSERVATIONS ▶

Impossible-to-get-out-of Situations

- Someone shoulders you when you pass them in the hall.
- You hear another young person telling some friends what a punk you are.
- A teacher who has been picking on you all year tells you to go to the office for no good reason.
- A smaller, younger person you have picked on in the past tells a teacher that you threw something at him or her.
- An older, larger person threatens to beat you up after school.
- Someone who has picked on you throws a carrot at you that hits you in the head during lunch.
- The liaison police officer in your school says that you're being watched really carefully so you'd better watch your step.
- Another young person gets in your face during a passing period and begins poking you in the chest with a finger.
- A group of young people surrounds you and starts calling you names.
- You are walking down the hall and hear two other young people arguing. You run over to watch and see that one of them is your best friend.
- Two other young people have repeatedly tripped you in the hall or tried to throw your books on the floor as a joke.

Response Options

- Talk it out with an adult you can trust.
- Express yourself in an assertive manner by telling the other person, "When you do this, I feel . . ."
- Tell yourself: "Right now, it is not safe to respond to this person or this situation. I need to talk to someone about how I feel in this situation before I react."
- Tell yourself: "I am scared here and don't feel I have a way out of this situation. I need to get to a safe place and think about how to deal with this situation."
- Tell yourself: "I don't need to get in any more trouble right now. I can avoid trouble by staying out of it."
- Tell yourself: "I feel trapped and confused about how to respond. I don't want this person to do this to me anymore. I don't deserve to be treated like this."
- Tell yourself: "I don't need to get angry or blow up right now. In fact, if I do blow up, it will get me into bigger trouble."
- Tell yourself: "I can be honest and express my feelings in an assertive manner, even though this person may not change how he or she deals with me."
- Tell yourself: "This is not my issue, but I think the best way for me to help is to explain what I see going on and say what would help me if I were in this situation."
- Tell yourself: "The way I'm being treated seems so unfair. I want these people to respect me and to include me. First, I will get safe, and then, I will talk with some friends to get ideas on how to deal with this situation."
- Say: "When you say these things, I feel frustrated and embarrassed. I want you to either talk with me about what's going on for you or not say anything."

91.
Sexual Bullying:
I Hear "No," I Believe "No"

Recommended
ages: 10 +

Phase 3

GOALS	■ Group members increase their ability to hear "no" and to stop.
	■ Group members increase their awareness of their personal boundaries.

DESCRIPTION

Group members discuss appropriate responses to "no" or "stop" and what gets in the way of those responses.

MATERIALS NEEDED

None.

DIRECTIONS

Discuss and list on the chalkboard or newsprint situations in which someone else would say "no" or "stop." Some situations could be:

■ The other person is being called a name.
■ The other person is offended by sexually inappropriate talk.
■ The other person does not like how he or she is being touched.
■ The other person is tired of being teased.

Ask participants to talk about how they could respond if someone said "no" or "stop" to them. List both positive and negative options on the chalkboard or newsprint. Then go through the options one at a time and have participants rate on a scale of one to ten (one being the least likely and ten being the most likely) how likely they are to respond using that option. Review the results, asking questions such as the following:

■ Which response seems the most likely to be used in these situations?
■ Which response seems the least likely to be used in these situations?
■ What responses seem to be similar in rating?

Note that any response that does not respect the other person's request to stop is an inappropriate response. Then ask if there were any inappropriate responses that were rated likely to be used. Ask what gets in the way of using appropriate responses, and write the barriers on the chalkboard or newsprint.

Discuss at length positive ways to deal with these barriers. Explain that the goal of this activity is not only to hear "no" but to also believe it.

THINGS TO THINK ABOUT

Talking about issues even remotely related to sexuality can feel uncomfortable. Most young people are not used to talking about sex in an open, honest manner. However, it is very important that these issues be addressed overtly. Being the target of sexual bullying can be devastating to young people.

You could rate the responses in the activity again at a later time to see if information was retained.

MY OBSERVATIONS

92.
Face-to-face

**Recommended
ages:** 10 +

Phase 3

GOALS ▶
- Group members understand the effects of their bullying behaviors on others.
- Group members gain empathy for the people they have bullied.
- Group members take responsibility for their own behaviors.

DESCRIPTION ▶
A facilitated discussion occurs at which two or three students who have been bullied are present. These visitors to the group share their perspectives and reactions to having been bullied.

MATERIALS NEEDED ▶
Circle of Courage talking piece.

DIRECTIONS ▶
Use the Circle of Courage process (see page 35) in an adapted "fish bowl" form. Introduce the guests to the group members. The guests sit just outside of the group and observe how group members respond to statements presented by the facilitator. The facilitator asks the group to respond to the following:

- Describe one situation in which you used bullying behaviors.
- Describe what you believe was the reason(s) for using these behaviors.
- Identify at least two feelings you had when bullying the other person.
- Describe what you believe were the feelings and concerns of the person you were bullying.
- Describe what tools you would use and changes you would make in behaviors if a similar situation occurred.
- If you could say something to the person you bullied, what would it be?
- If there were one thing that would be helpful for you to know from this person, what would it be?

After group members have had their chance to discuss this information, the guests then are asked to come into the circle. They are asked to respond to the following:

- Describe a situation during which someone was bullying you.
- How has this experience affected you at home, in school, in the community?
- Describe what you heard being shared by the group members.
- What would be helpful for the group members to understand?

The group members are then asked, "What is one thing you learned from this process or from what was said during this session?"

Debrief separately with the guests and with the group members. Take particular note of how the guests seem to be faring emotionally. Ask them: "What did you notice about the time together?" "In your mind, what was the most significant thing that happened?" "What was the most intense or difficult thing to hear or see?" "What did you do to deal with this?" Explain that they each may experience this time in a different way. Let them know their reactions and feelings are normal. Provide them with your work number should they want to talk more about their experience.

THINGS TO THINK ABOUT ▶

This can be a powerful and challenging activity and should only be done well into the third phase of a group, when trust has been well established.

Having people who are not the direct targets of the group members but who have experienced bullying behavior provide their perspective gives an opportunity for group members to better understand the impact of their behavior on others. Young people who have used bullying behavior often rely on objectification of their targets in order to continue their behavior. When their targets become real, personal, and able to present their perspectives, group members more clearly understand the effects. However, it is critical that you, as the facilitator, structure the discussion and facilitate the process to provide a safe atmosphere. Have your goals, methods, and process clearly in mind before conducting this activity.

There should be some criteria for selecting these guests. It can help to equalize the feeling of power imbalance if the guests are older and have a greater maturity level than the group members. The guests should also have demonstrated some growth in addressing their own related issues. They should receive a brief orientation to the group before they come, of course.

Debriefing is essential. This follow-up must be done with special sensitivity toward the group members since they have, in all probability, become increasingly vulnerable. It is important to help them look for ways to take care of themselves since they may be experiencing difficult feelings.

There will be a tendency for one or two group members to be unable to accept the guests' perspectives. Avoid power struggles with these members and look for ways to acknowledge their views. Avoid putting these members down or separating them. In the debriefing process, try to discuss their concerns.

This type of a meeting can also escalate tension and anxiety in the group. Be clear with group members that the purpose for this meeting is to help them understand the effects of their past behavior, and that this process has often been helpful to similar groups in the past.

MY OBSERVATIONS ▶

93.
Impact Web

GOALS ▶	■ Group members understand that hurting one person affects many others. ■ Group members understand that their behavior affects others. ■ Group members increase their ability to empathize.
DESCRIPTION ▶	Group members diagram the effects of their behavior.
MATERIALS NEEDED ▶	A copy of the Who Was Affected? worksheet (page 219) for each participant and pencils.
DIRECTIONS ▶	Explain to group members that whenever someone hurts another person, many people are affected by the behavior. Tell them that they are going to diagram a situation in which they have either physically or emotionally hurt another person. Pass out the Who Was Affected? worksheet and pencils. Tell group members to write in each of the three circles that extend from the "Me" circle the name of a person who was affected by their behavior, either by seeing or hearing that the behavior took place. Have them continue to do this until all the circles on the page contain a name.

Ask the group members to discuss the impact of their behavior, using questions such as the following:

■ How many people could one behavior affect?
■ What might be some of the positive ways people were affected by this behavior?
■ What are some of the negative ways people were affected by this behavior?
■ Could this behavior affect how others view you?
■ In what way?
■ Could this behavior affect how people who don't even know you view you?

MY OBSERVATIONS ▶

_____

_____

_____

Who Was Affected?

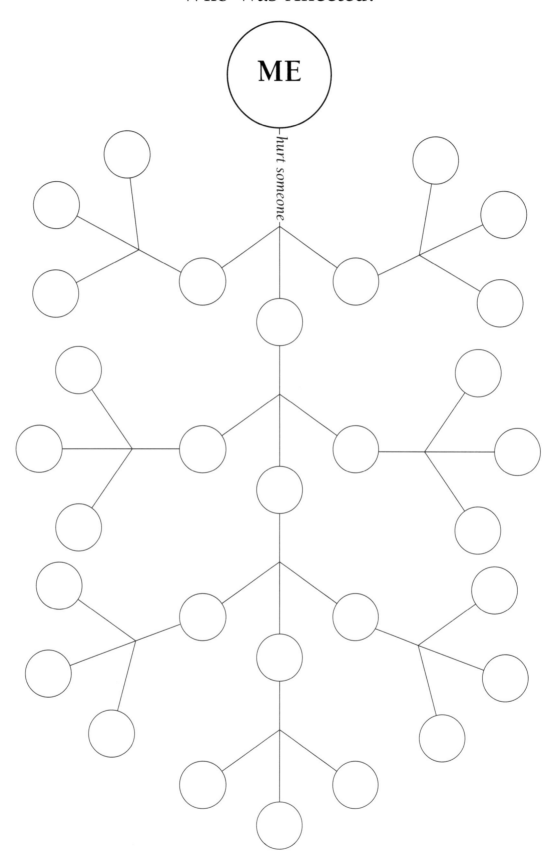

ME

hurt someone

94.
Journey of Peace

Recommended
ages: 10 +

Phase 3

GOALS	■ Group members have an image of the word *peace*. ■ Group members begin to understand that peace is something to strive for.
DESCRIPTION ▶	Group members, either individually or in pairs, chart journeys of peace they will begin in the first fifteen minutes of this session and continue in the first fifteen minutes of the next session, with an option to continue for as many sessions after that as the facilitator wishes.
MATERIALS NEEDED ▶	Paper, pencils, crayons, colored pencils, markers, and scissors.
DIRECTIONS ▶	Explain that at the beginning or end of this session and the next (plus up to two more sessions if you would like), group members will go on a journey of peace. Explain that people have different ways to acquire wisdom. Native Americans have a tradition of vision quests, Aboriginal Australians have walkabouts, other people may have retreats. Their journey of peace is a way to acquire wisdom about how they can be more peaceful in their lives. They can make this journey alone or with another group member.

Ask participants to draw a map of the journey they are about to take. Have them include directions, obstacles, possible rewards, and things they pick up along the way. They do not need to write a story about this journey but must be able to describe it to the rest of the group. If two people are involved, both must agree on the map, and both must present their thoughts related to the journey's elements. The final destination of their journey is the teaching place—the place of mastery, the place from which they can pass the wisdom and knowledge learned to another person.

Have participants make stepping-stones to mark the lessons learned. They make the stones by cutting shapes out of paper and writing on them the lessons they learned.

Allow the group members plenty of time each session to develop this journey. It should overlap at least two sessions and optimally four sessions. The amount of time given to this activity should be around ten to fifteen minutes per session.

Ask participants to describe their journeys either at the end of each segment or at the end of the whole journey. Ask questions such as the following:

- What parts of your journey are new for you?
- Who is in charge of the journey?
- What are some of the peaceful things you picked up along the journey?
- Describe some of the lessons you marked on your stepping-stones.

THINGS TO THINK ABOUT ▶

You may wish to have participants place their stones either on the floor or on the walls of the room. This can provide encouragement and recognition of their progress. It also serves as a reminder of what they have learned.

Using this activity during the last fifteen minutes of the sessions allows you to use it as a time to summarize the progress each group member made throughout the program.

MY OBSERVATIONS ▶

_____

_____

_____

_____

_____

_____

_____

_____

_____

_____

_____

_____

95.
A Safe Place

GOAL	■ Group members have an identified place at school or other institution where they feel safe.
DESCRIPTION	The group develops a story together about a child who needs a safe place, then identifies a place at school or another institution where each participant feels safe.
MATERIALS NEEDED	None.
DIRECTIONS	Present two or three situations in which participants might feel unsafe. Ask them where they would go or whom they would talk to in these situations. Note that in many games there are places set aside in which players can stay safe: in tag, there is a free base; in soccer or basketball, the sidelines; in baseball, the bases. Ask questions such as the following:

- What makes a place safe?
- How does a place become safe?
- How do you know you are safe there?
- Is being safe a feeling or an action?
- Are there different ways of not feeling safe? (Not feeling safe at home alone might feel different than not feeling safe if a gang of people starts pushing you around.)
- When have you felt unsafe?
- What did you do to feel safe again? (Perhaps left the situation.)
- Whom did you talk to or see to help you feel safe?

Ask group members to name safe places they can go to. List these on the chalkboard or newsprint. Ask members to name safe people they can talk to. List these on the chalkboard or newsprint. Ask them to tell what they were thinking during a time when they were in an unsafe place. Finally, ask them to share what they could tell themselves when things seem scary. List the positive self-messages on the chalkboard or newsprint.

Ask group members to help you develop a story about a young person who is the same age as they are. Ask for a name for this person. If the group consists of both boys and girls, ask them what gender this person is. Otherwise, make the young person the same gender as the group. Tell them other young people have teased this person about many things. Ask them to think of some things this person might have gotten teased about. Then state that this young person always had a safe place to go at his home, where he felt protected from everyone who could tease him. He also had a good friend to talk to and an adult to hang out with and talk to, although not necessarily about the teasing.

Continue the story by saying that this young person got teased by the same classmate for a whole week, and soon he felt _____.

Ask the group to develop a list of feelings and thoughts that this person might have. Then ask them to name positive messages he could give himself instead. Write this list on the chalkboard or newsprint. When the story is done, have the group members draw this person and the person or the place he went to to feel safe.

Lead a discussion asking questions such as the following:

- Where in the school (or other institution) could you feel safe?
- Which people in the school (or other institution) could you safely talk with? (Allow participants to struggle with this part. Many of them may not have a safe place at the school, or many of them may minimize the need to feel safe at the school, particularly if they do not feel threatened.)
- Is there a difference between feeling safe at school (or other institution) and feeling safe at home?
- What is the difference?
- What sorts of things would help the school (or other institution) feel more safe?
- What strategies could be undertaken to make the school (or other institution) more safe?

THINGS TO THINK ABOUT ▶

Some group members may feel vulnerable if they admit to ever having been afraid. Guide the discussion so group members do not feel ashamed of having these thoughts and feelings.

Some group members may genuinely not sense that they have ever been unsafe. It might take a more threatening or higher level of violence for such group members to register a situation as being hurtful. Young people sometimes develop coping mechanisms and even callousness to violence to such an extent that they do not register it as a problem. Try to help them identify those times when they observed or experienced even a small amount of fear for safety for themselves or a friend. Use this as a baseline with them.

MY OBSERVATIONS ▶

_____

_____

_____

96.
Building a Community of Peace

Recommended ages: 10 +

Phase 3

GOAL

- Group members increase their understanding of what contributes to feelings of safety in a community.

DESCRIPTION

Each group member draws a different building in a city and lists within the building suggestions for carrying out peaceful actions pertinent to the activities of that building.

MATERIALS NEEDED

A piece of paper large enough for the entire group to draw on together and drawing materials.

DIRECTIONS

Ask group members to sit around a large piece of paper. Assign each of them one or two buildings to draw, such as the city hall, a bakery, a police station, a community center, a hardware store. When they have completed their drawing, explain that this is now their community. As a group, they are to develop ideas for creating a community of peace.

Emphasize to participants that they will undoubtedly want to feel safe within this community. Ask them to list within each building their suggestions for how the activities that occur in that building could promote peace. What things can help people feel safe? After they have completed their lists, ask them questions such as the following:

- What suggestions within each building do you think are doable?
- What similarities are there between the suggestions listed in the buildings?

Focus on the suggestions for peaceful action within one building. Ask the group members to give ideas for next steps that could be taken to make these actions happen.

Ask group members what is different about taking peaceful action. Ask them if they feel they have an opportunity to help carry out any of these suggestions. If they feel they are powerless to do anything, ask them to identify what it is that keeps them from being able to do anything.

Some group members will offer suggestions such as more security, more guns, and other violence-based approaches. No doubt, this activity will elicit responses that are based on legitimate fears and thoughts of insecurity. This will especially be true in the wake of well-publicized traumatic events in the community or nation. Nevertheless, encourage the group to focus on using peaceful means and behaviors to sustain peace in the community.

**MY
OBSERVATIONS** ▶

_____

_____

_____

_____

_____

_____

_____

_____

_____

_____

_____

_____

_____

_____

_____

_____

PHASE FOUR

101

Support Group Activities

For Teenagers Who Bully

A Leader's Manual
for Secondary Educators
and Other Professionals

97.
Accessing Support

GOALS

- Group members understand that support from others is something everybody needs.
- Group members identify people or places they can turn to for support.

DESCRIPTION

Group members create "access cards" that list people or places they can get support from and ways to go about getting the support.

MATERIALS NEEDED

A three-by-five-inch index card for each member of the group and pens or pencils.

DIRECTIONS

Discuss the concept of support, asking group members to share words and ideas about what *support* means to them. Ask them for examples. Develop a list, on the chalkboard or newsprint, of all the people who provide some sort of support to them. Develop a list of the types of support they receive from these people. Include money, emotional support, shelter, clothing, other types of gifts, intangible support, and so on. Ask questions such as the following:

- Do you ask certain people for support?
- If so, how do you ask?
- Do you just assume that certain people will give you support?
- When you feel unsafe, what kind of support do you want from others? When you feel scared? When you feel angry?
- Are there ways to get support without having to ask?
- Can you still get what you need this way?
- What are some examples of how this can happen?

Next, ask participants for examples of how they go about getting support. List the examples they offer on the chalkboard or newsprint. Examples might include just spending time with someone, or asking for support from a trusted friend or family member. Have the group members pair up and role-play situations in which they ask each other for some sort of support.

Give each member an index card. Have them write their names on the cards, and under their names list three people or places they feel they can get support. Have them then list the ways they would get this support (for instance, by asking, by visiting, or by calling this person). Have them share two of their options with the rest of the group. Ask questions such as the following:

- Are there similarities among the people group members mentioned?
- Are there similarities among the places group members would go for support?
- Were there any suggestions you could add to your own list?

Explain that they now have a card that can remind them of who to talk to or what to do when they feel they need to get support.

THINGS TO THINK ABOUT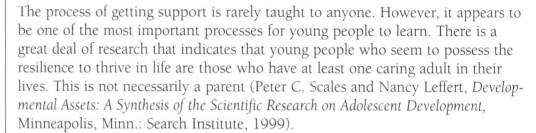

The process of getting support is rarely taught to anyone. However, it appears to be one of the most important processes for young people to learn. There is a great deal of research that indicates that young people who seem to possess the resilience to thrive in life are those who have at least one caring adult in their lives. This is not necessarily a parent (Peter C. Scales and Nancy Leffert, *Developmental Assets: A Synthesis of the Scientific Research on Adolescent Development*, Minneapolis, Minn.: Search Institute, 1999).

It may be challenging to convince group members that they need and should get support. Many boys feel considerable pressure to do everything on their own. Even though doing things on their own is frequently extremely hard for them to bear, it is also very hard for them to admit they need support, even to themselves. In addition, young men and women often believe they are invincible. They sometimes don't seem to buy that there is a need for anyone else in their lives and think they don't need to be connected to anyone. Selling the need for support can be a tough job for facilitators. Unfortunately, it often takes some traumatic experiences for young people to become aware that many others have experienced similar situations, and they can benefit by connecting with these people. Still, even the hard-core loner will usually understand, in time, that everybody needs support sometimes. Everybody has someone in their lives who really has provided some stability and support—otherwise, they wouldn't have made it as far as they have.

MY OBSERVATIONS

_____

_____

_____

_____

98.
Support Web

GOAL ▶

- Group members are able to identify people and places they can turn to for support.

DESCRIPTION ▶

Group members diagram their support networks.

MATERIALS NEEDED ▶

A sheet of paper for each group member, pencils, and crayons, colored pencils, or markers.

DIRECTIONS ▶

Explain that everybody deserves to have a network of support at school, at home, or wherever they are in their lives. It is easier to get support when you need it if you know where to go and whom you can get it from.

Give participants drawing materials. Give directions as follows:

1. Draw a circle centered at the top of the paper and, in it, write your name or the word *Me*.
2. Draw three lines from the top circle to three separate circles. In each of these three circles, write the name of a friend or family member whom you like to hang out with or whom you can talk to about problems. You might even label one of these circles "Myself."
3. Draw three more lines from the center circle a little farther out than the three circles you've already added. Again, add three more circles at the ends of these lines. In each of these circles, write things you do that help you feel good, safe, or happy. These could be things like playing a sport, watching a certain movie, listening to a certain song, playing cards, or shopping.
4. Draw three more lines from the center circle even farther out to three more circles. In each of these circles, write specific places you can go where it feels safe. These could be places in your home or in your community. It might be your closet, the basement, a friend's house, a place of worship, the arcade, a playground.
5. Shade with red those people, places, or activities that can be contacted, gone to, or done in an emergency.
6. Shade with yellow those people who can be contacted for simple questions or just to hang around with.
7. Finally, shade with blue the circles that are places you simply like to go or people you want to be around but don't have to let know about all the difficult and stressful concerns you have.

Ask the group members to discuss their webs to whatever degree they feel safe to do so. After some group members have shared their information, ask if they heard any similarities among the webs.

Summarize by emphasizing that having a support web, knowing whom to connect with or where to go, is important. Ask group members to think about what they have written in their webs today when they need to use their support system.

THINGS TO THINK ABOUT ▶

Try not to be discouraged if group members have difficulty with this activity. Our culture values independence highly, and reliance upon others is not typically emphasized. It may be difficult for group members to identify sources of support.

MY OBSERVATIONS ▶

_____

_____

_____

_____

_____

_____

_____

_____

_____

_____

_____

_____

_____

99.
Supportive Adults in My Life

Recommended ages: 10 +

Phase 4

GOALS ▶
- Group members increase their understanding of the support networks they have in their lives.
- Group members are able to increase the number of people to connect with when necessary.

DESCRIPTION ▶ Group members diagram their support network.

MATERIALS NEEDED ▶ Paper and pencils for each group member.

DIRECTIONS ▶ Have each group member draw a circle centered at the top of the page labeled "Me." From this circle, they should draw five lines, each with another circle on the end. In these circles, have them write the names of significant adults in their lives. Examples might include a parent, a sibling, a very close friend, a grandparent. Next have them draw five more lines from the center circle to five new circles one level beyond the first set. In the second set, they should write the names of adults they have contact with but to whom they feel less emotionally connected than the first set. Examples might include a coach, a teacher, a friend. Finally, have them draw five more lines from the center circle to five new circles beyond the rest. Have them write in these circles the names of adults they have some connection with, although minimal. Examples might include an acquaintance, a school administrator, a clergyperson.

Ask the group members to share their adult support systems. Ask questions such as the following:

- What qualities make your first tier of adult supports so special?
- Are there similar qualities among first-tier supports chosen by different group members? Among second-tier supports? Among third-tier supports?
- Are there some people farther out whom you wish were closer in?
- How do you relate differently to the closer adults than to the ones in the farther tiers?

Point out that it is important for them to understand which adults play a significant role in their lives. Knowing whom they can count on adds to a feeling of security.

Group members may have difficulty identifying adults who are significant to them. This is not to be confused with resistance. Even adults rarely undergo this process. Provide as many examples as possible. Sometimes it is easier for them if they can draw all the lines and circles before filling in any names.

_____

_____

_____

_____

_____

_____

_____

_____

_____

_____

_____

_____

_____

_____

_____

_____

_____

100.
What I Learned . . .

GOALS ▶
- Group members can name what they have learned.
- Group members develop postgroup plans.

DESCRIPTION ▶ Group members take turns talking in a Circle of Courage about what they have learned.

MATERIALS NEEDED ▶ Circle of Courage talking piece and a chalkboard or newsprint printed with the sentence "One thing I have learned in or from this group is . . ."

DIRECTIONS ▶ Have the group form a Circle of Courage (see page 35) and complete the sentence "One thing I have learned in or from this group is . . ." Have each group member respond as quickly and briefly as possible. Go around the circle as many times as possible within three minutes. Let the group know that most groups reach thirty different things they have learned, although one group was able to reach forty-five. You may want to write their contributions on the board.

After the group has completed the activity, ask them what themes they heard about what was learned during the group process.

Summarize what you have shared and observed.

THINGS TO THINK ABOUT ▶ Closing activities for groups like these can produce some anxiety. Group members often are just beginning to come together, and now you are reminding them that the end is near.

Sometimes group members' behavior gets worse toward the end of the program as they anticipate the loss of contact with people they have grown increasingly comfortable with.

MY OBSERVATIONS ▶

_____

_____

_____

_____

101.
Go-around Good-byes

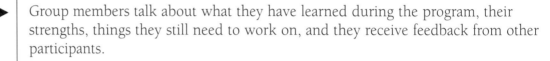

Recommended
ages: 10 +

Phase 4

GOALS ▶
- Group members internalize more deeply what they have learned.
- Group members better understand and build empathy toward others.

DESCRIPTION ▶
Group members talk about what they have learned during the program, their strengths, things they still need to work on, and they receive feedback from other participants.

MATERIALS NEEDED ▶
None.

DIRECTIONS ▶
Have group members sit in a circle. Ask for a volunteer to respond to the following statements:

- One thing I learned (or one way I benefited) from being in this group is . . .
- One thing that I still need to work on is . . .
- One strength I have is . . .

Next, have group members take turns responding to these statements regarding the member who volunteered:

- One way this group member has benefited me or the group is . . .
- One thing that would be useful for this group member to work on some more is . . .
- One strength about this group member is . . .

After each group member has shared his or her messages to the volunteer, the volunteer gets "the last word." This is his or her opportunity to share something further, talking directly to the facilitator or other group members. This person lets the group know when he or she is finished with the last word.

Repeat this process until everybody in the group has had an opportunity to be the focus.

Ask the group to reflect on what this process was like.

The ending of a group process can cause group members some anxiety. Even the anticipation of the end raises some feelings. There may be an increase in inappropriate behaviors, due mostly to continued difficulty in appropriately expressing feelings.

Sometimes it is helpful to precede this activity with a discussion on loss. A sample discussion question could be: how does it feel when you lose contact with someone because of a death or because he or she moved away? This provides group members the chance to explore negative feelings in a structured way and to end their contact with fellow group members in a positive manner. Group members have rarely ended relationships in a constructive way.

This is a good time to give them all the credit for the work they've done and to let them know that their participation will help future group members. In a way, parts of themselves have been left with you and each group member.

Group members sometimes have difficulty identifying suggestions for someone else in the group to focus on in the future. It may help if you role-model some examples.

If you used Activity 45, Interviewing Someone with Peaceful Behavior Experience, remember to review the interviews either in this session or one of the final sessions.

MY OBSERVATIONS ▶

_____

_____

_____

_____

_____

_____

_____

_____

_____

_____

Hazelden Publishing and Educational Services is a division of the Hazelden Foundation, a not-for-profit organization. Since 1949, Hazelden has been a leader in promoting the dignity and treatment of people afflicted with the disease of chemical dependency.

The mission of the foundation is to improve the quality of life for individuals, families, and communities by providing a national continuum of information, education, and recovery services that are widely accessible; to advance the field through research and training; and to improve our quality and effectiveness through continuous improvement and innovation.

Stemming from that, the mission of this division is to provide quality information and support to people wherever they may be in their personal journey—from education and early intervention, through treatment and recovery, to personal and spiritual growth.

Although our treatment programs do not necessarily use everything Hazelden publishes, our bibliotherapeutic materials support our mission and the Twelve Step philosophy upon which it is based. We encourage your comments and feedback.

The headquarters of the Hazelden Foundation are in Center City, Minnesota. Additional treatment facilities are located in Chicago, Illinois; New York, New York; Plymouth, Minnesota; St. Paul, Minnesota; and West Palm Beach, Florida. At these sites, we provide a continuum of care for men and women of all ages. Our Plymouth facility is designed specifically for youth and families.

For more information on Hazelden, please call **1-800-257-7800.** Or you may access our World Wide Web site on the Internet at **www.hazelden.org.**